CULTURAL EXCHANGE . . .

Mindy blushed. "I'm sorry, you didn't understand. I drink with my mouth, smell with my nose, uh, see with my eyes, and hear with my ears."

Mork shook his head in dismay. "You primitive beings lead exhausting lives."

"Primitive." Mindy felt angry for all human beings. "What makes us primitive, because we don't drink with our fingers?"

"You don't understand living forms," Mork said. "Look, how you cage the plants and you eat animals and you kill each other—"

Mindy quickly interrupted. She was made sad by this list. "Your planet doesn't do any of those things?"

"Not since two *bill-krells*."

"How do you eat?"

"We eat plant leavings."

Mindy was confused. "You eat dead leaves?"

"Nap, nap. We eat the colored extrusions."

"You mean, flowers? You eat flowers?"

"And coffee, of course."

"But coffee and flowers don't have any nourishment," Mindy said.

Mork shook his head in disapproval. "And you say you're not a primitive life-form?"

Henderson Production Company, Inc.

and

Miller-Milkis Productions, Inc.

in association with Paramount Television

Present

MORK & MINDY

Created by

Garry K. Marshall
Dale McRaven
and
Joe Glauberg

"MORK: HOUR SPECIAL"
written by Dale McRaven

"MORK MOVES IN"
written by Lloyd Turner and Gordon Mitchell

"MORK RUNS AWAY"
written by April Kelly

Ralph Church

MORK & MINDY

PUBLISHED BY POCKET BOOKS NEW YORK

Another *Original* publication of POCKET BOOKS

 POCKET BOOKS, a Simon & Schuster division of
GULF & WESTERN CORPORATION
1230 Avenue of the Americas, New York, N.Y. 10020

ISBN: 0-671-82729-4

First Pocket Books printing January, 1979

10 9 8 7 6 5 4 3 2 1

Trademarks registered in the United States and other countries.

Interior design by Catherine Carucci.

Printed in the U.S.A.

MORK & MINDY

* * *

1

It had started like any other day on the planet Ork, only today Mork had been sent a special request to appear before the White Desk. On Ork you never knew what this could mean. For Mork it usually meant punishment.

Mork would have been nervous about being called before the White Desk except that Orkans don't feel nervous the way Earthlings do. But Mork was worried in the way that Orkans do feel scared. He couldn't keep his finger, or what he would call his *bloink*, from twitching. A twitching finger was a sure sign he was scared—*if* Orkans *could* be scared. He had already sent all the objects in the room flying because of his nervous *bloink*. Orkans can do just about everything with their right index finger, from drinking with them, to ironing shirts.

Soon, an enormous figure appeared on the wall behind the White Desk. But Mork hadn't noticed his large leader at all. He was too busy arguing with himself. "Boy, I must be really in trouble. Called before the White Desk *again*. But what did

I do?" Mork's face glowered and his voice became deep and scary: "The solar lander! You painted a mustache on it." Mork looked innocent. "But Orson doesn't know *I* did that."

As the fat shadow seemed to shimmer and enlarge, it spoke. "Mork!"

"Oh, boy, now he does." Mork turned with exaggerated casualness. "Good morning, Orson," he said cheerfully. He was carefully standing at attention as he had been taught at school when dealing with authority.

"Orson!" The fat shadow spoke with Orkian sarcasm, which sounded just like Orkian anger. This was a leader to respect. And he was no fool.

"Sure, you call me Orson to my face, but no sooner do I turn my back and you call me 'Fatso,' 'Rocketship Thighs,' 'Laser Breath,' and 'Star Tush'!" There was hurt in the voice and it was enough to make Mork solemn.

Mork lowered his brows so much, in an attempt to look solemn, that he had to use his hand to move them up again. Always trying to look on the cheery side, he said, "I was hoping you'd put all that behind you." Mork laughed, but it was an imitation of the laughter he heard when monitoring other planets where human beings still told jokes. "Ha! Ha! Ha!" He sounded like he was a duck in pain.

Orson raised his finger, a very serious gesture on Ork. He had a very little sense of humor, like most Orkans.

"Oops." Mork covered his mouth. "Sorry." He realized he had done wrong again.

"Do you see what I mean?" Orson said. "These constant displays of humor are illegal on Ork. *And* we don't like them. All emotion is unacceptable." Orson sighed. He liked Mork, but he just wasn't the same as other Orkans.

"Yes," Mork agreed. "We are a dull lot." He tried to keep all emotion from his voice.

"Emotions have been discarded for the good of the race. And you constantly make jokes. I'm afraid that won't do." Orson was rubbing his hands together, except for his right index finger, which stuck up in the air like a carpenter's sore thumb. "Well, I have a little assignment that just might straighten you up." Orson felt it was worth a try. One last chance for Mork to prove he was a good Orkan.

"Uh-oh!" Mork covered his face with his arms, a traditional gesture of Orkian fear. Showing fear is considered a misdemeanor. This was a serious business. He was sure of that.

Orson ignored him. It was the only sensible thing to do. "There's an insignificant planet on the far side of the galaxy. From the fragmented reports we have on the people there, they are . . . well . . ."

"Real *nimnuls*?" Mork suggested, using an archaic Orkian insult for which there is no penalty, although the desire to insult is against the law.

"Exactly," Orson said. "That's why I think you'll fit in there, Mork." Orson felt better for being so honest.

"Thank you, you're too kind," Mork said. Orson hadn't, in Orkian terms, insulted Mork; he had merely noticed his character. "What's the name of the hell-hole you're sending me to?"

"Earth."

"Earth?" Mork was about to show how happy he was but stopped himself just in time. Instead, he said, "I was on Earth once, not more than three *krells* ago. I went to get a specimen for biology class, but he was too small and I had to throw him back. I loved that place."

Orson would have been furious, he might even have raised his *bloink* in anger, but he was law-abiding. "Well, don't enjoy it too much. It's not a vacation. We want to learn all we can about primitive societies. Your mission is to report back to me—mentally, please, not in person. You report back to me about the things you learn there. And remember this is a serious mission."

Mork stood up straight, feeling illegal pride. "You can count on me, Orson. DEE, DEE and EEE —Dedicated, Diligent, and Efficient. Farewell, Chief." Mork grabbed his ears with his hands and did something that would have hurt an Earthling. He twisted his ears like they were dials, and at the same time said, *"Na-No, Na-No."* These were special words that every Orkan learned at a very early age. In fact, an Orkian baby said them before any other words—even Mama and Dadda.

Orson also twisted his ears with exaggerated politeness, and *also* said, *"Na-No, Na-No."* It was pretty funny coming from such a serious shadow, if you saw it as an Earthling. But for these two, it was no more painful than a handshake and most acceptable as a friendly farewell.

***

2

On Earth, in Boulder, Colorado, U.S.A., it was spring and a beautiful night. The sky was clear and there was a full moon lighting the trees. The crickets and nightbirds were keeping up a pleasant musical song for Mindy and her date, Bill. They were out on their third date. They had had a nice dinner and had driven to a beautiful rise where they could look at the lights of the city. It was romantic and isolated.

"I love this spot," Bill said. "So distant, so removed from humanity." He was a good-looking blond, twenty-two years old, with light blue eyes and full lips. Some girls thought he was "real cute." But Mindy wasn't sure of his chin. It was a little weak and her grandmother always said you couldn't trust weak-chinned men. But that was the foolishness of the older generation, Mindy told herself. Her generation knew enough to judge people on more than just their looks.

As for Mindy, she was above criticism by grandmothers. She had long, straight, shining brown hair, clear, honest eyes, and a lean figure that Orkans used to call a real *binzel*. But using that word nowadays might get you exiled to Earth. You weren't supposed to notice, let alone like such things on Ork.

But at that moment, Mindy knew nothing about Ork and was concentrating on Bill and the beautiful scenery.

"It is beautiful," Mindy agreed, forgetting about Bill's weak chin.

"Especially now"—Bill's voice was whispery, gentle—"when the bird of night has covered the sky with her wings of darkness and solitude."

"Bill," Mindy said with surprise, "that's very poetic." They were in an old Jeep that had no top and both had their heads back to look at the stars, which were twinkling in the sky with special brightness. They could see the Big Dipper, the North Star, Orion, and the Little Dipper.

But Bill wasn't interested in the stars. He pressed his advantage. "The reason I enjoy taking you out, Mindy, is that you don't force me into playing that virile, stud macho role, you know?"

"I'm glad you feel that way. Men shouldn't feel inhibited about expressing their poetic side." She was glad that she had gotten this chance to praise Bill's sensitivity. He was a big change from her usual dates and she wanted to be sure to encourage him to continue being lyrical and serious.

"You know what I see when I look at the sky?" Bill said. "Individual points of desolate, unloved light, so lonely because they can never touch."

Mindy was touched. "How sad."

"And sometimes"—Bill leaned forward—"I see the night sky as a woman tastefully adorned with brilliant sequins. Oh, the Milky Way is a little garish, but it's necessary because"—Bill turned in Mindy's direction and his voice became husky— "it covers her thighs." And with that Bill reached for Mindy's leg, shoved his face at her, and tried to kiss her passionately. So much for poetry!

Mindy was very surprised, but she reacted quickly. "Get away from me!" she said as she tried to push him away. But Bill went wild, and he wouldn't take no for an answer. He grabbed for Mindy as she tried to fight him off with all her strength.

Bill was not a fellow who could take a hint. "You love it!" he yelled. "I read you like a book!" he cried. And the struggle continued.

In desperation, Mindy grabbed a bunch of his hair and pulled him away.

Bill, wincing with pain, but unwilling to give up, said, "But you put up a great front."

"Don't ever do that again!" Mindy yelled. "Even if my dress is on fire. I'd rather burn to death."

"Hey!" Bill was red-faced from embarrassment, anger, and the pain of his hair-lift. "What's the matter with you? Three whole dates of my shy and poetic bit. Now let's get it on!"

Mindy was out of breath and angry. Very angry.

"So it was just an act, huh? Well, I don't find it so easy to jump from poetry to the bump!" she yelled.

While all this was going on, Mork was traveling from Ork to Earth. If anyone at all had been watching the sky that night, they would certainly have spotted a giant, brilliantly white four-foot-long egg that had drifted from the very stars that had been so romantic.

If Bill and Mindy hadn't been so busy fighting, they would have noticed it land twenty feet behind them. Even the whirring of its motors—a sound like a toy ambulance siren—was drowned out by their argument.

As the egg settled on land, the top of it cracked and fell away. Then quickly the whole structure fell open and Mork came out stretching like a newborn chick. But Mindy and Bill were still going at it.

"Three dates," Mindy was yelling, "and you think you have a right to attack me like a-a-a Thanksgiving turkey!" she finished.

"Oh, I love it when you talk dirty," Bill said, refusing to listen to her rejection.

Even if Mindy and Bill were too busy to hear the Flying Egg, Mork could hardly miss them. But after looking at the couple briefly, he turned away and looked up at the sky. A smaller Flying Egg was descending to Earth and immediately landed. He opened it and took out a small steel box with a handle.

"Only one suitcase?" he mumbled. And then he complained, "That's only half my luggage."

He shook his hand heavenward. "You *nimnuls!*" He then put his hand over his mouth. "They might be listening. I must behave."

While Mork was claiming his luggage, Mindy was still having her troubles. Just when she thought the situation was under control, Bill lunged again. But she grabbed his hair again and pulled, saying, "Look, I'm no prude, but you're out of line."

Bill clenched his teeth so he wouldn't scream from the pain. "I love a girl with spunk," he said slowly through his teeth.

She held onto his hair, not wanting to take unnecessary chances. "I liked you better when you were ineffectual. After tonight, I don't like you at all."

Bill held still, peering up at Mindy, and answered, "Good point! I think I should take you home. Because I respect you."

"I think I'd better drive just to make sure we get to our respective homes, still respecting each other." She let go of his hair and got out of the Jeep to move to his side. Bill immediately turned on the ignition.

"If that's the way you feel, why don't you walk home!" And he quickly drove the car out, leaving Mindy stranded and yelling after a disappearing car.

While all this was going on, Mork was busy changing from his spacesuit into Earth clothing. He had come prepared. As he struggled with a suit, shirt, and tie, Mork thought it was amazing that humans were still so primitive that they couldn't make a single unit of material to cover the whole body. Instead, they were in pieces, like a broken egg.

He had no trouble getting his five-foot-five frame (all Orkans are five-feet, five-inches tall, except for government Orkans, who are lengthened to six feet when elected) into the pants, shirt, tie, and jacket. That was easy. But what he didn't know was how to wear them. So he made the mistake of putting his jacket, shirt, and tie on backward. And since the jacket was black, and since he was covered completely in front except for the white of his collar, he emerged from behind the trees and looked just like a priest. So when he appeared in front of Mindy, who was furiously yelling after Bill, and said, "*Syfnid,* Earthling," she could only assume that Mork *was* actually a priest.

"Father, what are you doing here?" Mindy was surprised but was too angry to give it much thought.

"This is where I was dropped off," Mork said with a vague gesture in the direction of the broken Flying Egg, which had disappeared.

"Well, I got dropped off, too," Mindy said, looking in the direction of Bill's escape. "You wouldn't believe what happened to me! He took *my* car. I'm glad to have someone to walk into town with who I can trust. This isn't a confession or anything, but I had only three crummy dates with the guy and he takes my car and makes me walk."

Mork's eyebrows lowered. "Very interesting," he said in the normal Orkian voice that sounds like a tape recorder speeded up. He took out a pad. "May I take notes?"

"I don't know where he gets off," Mindy went on angrily, not noticing that Mork was writing with his finger. "I mean, the first two dates he wanted pizza, with everything. Third date, no pizza—he just wants *everything*."

Mork found all this very strange. Apparently, on Earth, it was rude to want pizza, a substance that must be like *grebbles*, Orkian money. Or perhaps it was a fuel. That must be it, since he took her vehicle.

Mork was kept so busy taking notes of Mindy's angry speech that he didn't pay attention to his surroundings as they walked to town. Nor did Mindy notice that other pedestrians were pointing and giggling at the sight of Mork with his jacket on backward, and his finger scribbling furiously on the pad. Mork was glad when they arrived at Mindy's because he had almost worn his nail all the way down.

* * *

3

Mindy led Mork up to a large, rambling, old Victorian house, with lots of odd angles and charming windows. It was newly painted white, with a gingerbread trim, and had been divided into apartments. They climbed up the wide staircase to Mindy's floor.

"Well, here we are," Mindy said, opening the door. "Thanks for walking me home, Father. I'm sorry I didn't give you a chance to talk, but I was so furious."

"*Nap, nap,*" Mork said, which is the pleasant way of saying no in Orkian. There are seventeen different no's in their language, six of them illegal. "My pleasure. I was sent here to learn, you know."

Mindy really looked at Mork for the first time. There was something about him that was strange. But she couldn't put her finger on it. It wasn't just that Mork's voice was unusually high-pitched and that he spoke very fast, or even that his suit fit funny. She still hadn't seen the back of it!

"Is there anything I can offer you?" she asked, trying to be polite.

"I'll have a glass of water if it's not too precious." When Mindy looked puzzled, Mork quickly added, "If it is, I'll have a quart of oil instead."

Mindy laughed, surprised that a priest was so hip, but she answered, "No, I can spring for a glass of water."

Mork's finger pointed up in the air, the traditional Orkian gesture of thought. "Spring—water. Ah! You are being humorous. Ha! Ha! Ha!" he quacked, throwing his head back with his mouth open.

Mindy had already turned toward the kitchen and didn't notice this strange behavior. "Hey! I've got a better idea. How about some iced tea?" she asked.

Mork nodded yes, but was more interested in the plants resting on Mindy's bookcase. He whispered gently while holding one leaf against his index finger. "Are they treating you well here?" he queried sincerely.

Mindy couldn't help overhear him as she returned with the iced tea. "Oh, you talk to plants, too?"

"Only to the old ones. They're good listeners."

Mindy put the iced tea on her coffee table and sat down on the couch. She just couldn't figure it out. Something was wrong. But when Mork turned his back to her, as he walked around the sofa, Mindy knew! "Your—your suit is on backward!"

Mork grabbed his head and looked down, embarrassed. "It is? I feel like such a clone," he apologized, since on Ork, though they could make perfect copies of themselves, they had been having problems with the brain cells in the index finger.

"If you're not a priest, who are you?" Mindy asked, now afraid she was involved with a kook.

"I'm Mork from Ork," was the answer. And Mork pulled himself up to his five-feet, five-inches and saluted this beautiful Earthling.

"Ork?" she repeated in a daze.

"Ork is a planet. You follow the Big Dipper until it comes to a dead end. Then you hang an up—"

Mindy imitated Mork's hand gesture, which was that he pointed down when he said up.

"Or is that down?" Mork asked. "It doesn't matter. In hyper-space it's hard to tell."

Mindy shook herself and took action. She began to climb off the couch, terrified. What a night. First she was attacked by her date. Now this. But she didn't want to let him know she was frightened. So far he hadn't hurt her. Now, if she could only humor him. "Right," she said, pretending that Mork was making sense. "I have a poor sense of direction myself. So," she said with a perky tone, "you're from Outer Space, eh?" What else could she say?

"Yes," Mork answered blandly. After all, it was no news to him. In fact, he was so intent in his new mission, he never even noticed Mindy's strange actions. "Mind if I take a picture?" he asked without waiting for an answer. "The clones love getting postcards." Mork aimed his finger at Mindy, who was still climbing off of the couch and now began to fall.

As she struggled to hang on, Mork triggered his camera-finger and the room flashed with light. Mindy, astonished, slid down again. "How did you do that?" was all she could say.

Mork pointed to the nail on his middle finger. "It's my Instamatic nail. You can get them for less than thirty *brandels*. Putting it on is a little painful, though." Mork ignored Mindy on the floor. After all, this could be normal Earthling behavior.

Mork looked down and saw his tea. "Ah," he said, and, with no feeling, put two fingers in the glass. In a second, the iced tea disappeared. "Mustn't gulp." he said, smiling. "The pause that refreshes," he quoted, and he bent his fingers while making a loud burping noise.

Mindy was staring so hard that her eyes began to hurt. "You drank that with your finger," she said, mostly to convince herself of what she had seen.

"Of course," Mork said, then suspected that something was wrong. Perhaps Earthlings drank differently. "How do *you* drink liquids?" he asked in his best interview manner.

"With"—Mindy's hand strayed to her lips—"my mouth."

Mork thought about that. "Then how do you talk and drink at the same time? Must be drool city."

Now Mindy was *really* scared. Either she was crazy, or she was alone with a bizarre, possibly dangerous, lunatic. "Look," she said, her voice trembling, "whoever you are, you can't scare me. There's no such thing as a man from Outer Space. I don't know how you did those tricks, but just keep your distance or I'm going to scream like you've never heard anybody scream."

"I've never heard *anybody* scream," Mork answered in his fast, high-toned voice. "Is that another way of saying thanks?" Orkans have four ways of saying thank you, so Mork thought his guess was a good one.

Mindy readied herself to yell, but a knock on the

door stopped her. "Ah!" she said, leaping from the couch and running to the door. "Here's help already," she said, opening the door triumphantly.

Hovering in the doorway was another Flying Egg from Ork. Mindy put her hand on the door to steady herself and slowly collapsed, staring at the white object. This couldn't be happening to her.

"My lost luggage," Mork said matter-of-factly. "That's *goomba* because all my casual clothes are in it." At the doorway, the egg opened by lifting its top and Mork removed another steel box with a handle.

"*Scrim, scrim,* scram," he said to get the egg to leave. When it just stayed in place, Mork was irritated.

"Take a hike," Mork said. After a moment he realized his mistake. "Oh, everybody expects a tip these days," Mork mumbled, taking out the blue marbles that are coin money on Ork. Sand are the big bills. The egg said, "*Pah-poo,*" one of the formal Orkian thank-yous, closed its top, and whirred away.

Mindy, still slumped by the doorway, tried to talk, but she had to clear her throat first. "You actually are—you came from up there?" Mindy pointed skyward.

Mork took her arm and moved it slightly. "Actually, I'm from over there." He moved her arm back to the original position. Then he explained: "That direction is not a good neighborhood. Lots of mumps. I wouldn't even go there in an eclipse."

"An alien," Mindy mumbled, getting up. "An alien," she repeated, letting this incredible idea sink in. "You're not going to hurt me?" she quickly added.

"Hurt?" Mork shook his head, disappointed.

"Damaging other life-forms is against our nature. It's unthinkable. I wouldn't harm a *boz* on your *yin*." Mork peered at Mindy's neck. "Though you don't seem to have a *boz*."

Mindy walked to the other side of her couch and took a good look at Mork. He was, of course, five-feet, five-inches tall, with blue eyes, questioning eyebrows, a wide nose that was a little twisted, and thin lips. His body was powerfully built, and he held it very erect and proud. He wore his hair fairly long and looked very much in fashion, except that Mindy noticed his jacket had no buttons.

"I've met a man from space," Mindy said, no longer afraid and very excited. She almost felt flattered. But she was speechless.

***

4

Mindy sat there and stared, awed by Mork. This was the beginning of a long adventure, she realized. She had been chosen, out of all humanity, to be the first woman to meet a man from space.

"Just think of me as a new friend," Mork said, breaking the silence. "Ah! It occurs to me that we haven't been formally introduced. A formal introduction is at hand." Mork put his finger to his lips and a trumpet sound came out. He dropped to one knee. "I'm Mork from Ork."

"I'm Mindy McConnell." Mindy, a little embarrassed, made a feeble noise like a trumpet.

Mork stepped forward stiffly and extended his hand, spreading his index and middle fingers apart from the pinky and ring fingers. Mindy puzzled over this for a moment and then imitated him. That was a first-meeting Orkian handshake, quite different from the twisting-ear departure sign.

Mork approved of her handshake. "Ah, I like a firm *ribbit*. That shows character."

"Well, thank you. Uh, how do you say 'thank you' in your language?"

"*Pah-poo, klangst, tuppy*, and *hooey-goo*."

"You have four ways of saying thank you?"

"Of course. *Pah-poo* is for lower-life forms, *klangst* is to fill time, *tuppy* is for equals, and *hooey-goo* is said only to children."

"I just can't believe this is happening!" Mindy said, her eyes shining with delight. "I'm talking to an alien! Do you realize what a momentous occasion in the history, well, in the history of the whole world this is? Everyone will be astounded."

"*Boo, boo,*" Mork said, using one of the legal no's in Orkian. *Nap, nap* wouldn't have been correct because it is for social no's. *Boo, boo* is a business term. "My mission here is only to observe. I can only do that by being one of you. A face in the crowd. And that should be easy. I fit right in."

Mindy tried not to laugh. "Not really," she said gently.

Mork was surprised. "No?"

"No." Mindy nodded firmly.

"Are you sure?"

"I'm sure. I'll tell you what. I'm as interested in your planet and in you as you are in us. I can teach you how to act 'Earthling' and you can teach me about Ork. Is that a deal?"

"A fair exchange. We'll formally close the deal." Mork squeezed his chest. He seemed to actually tighten his rib cage by a few inches. In fact, Orkans, since they have no heart or lungs, can narrow their bodies in this fashion. How much one can do this is, indeed, their only athletic competition. "*Kerkle,*" Mork said, the appropriate phrase when making this gesture. Indeed, the chest-squeezing games are called *Kerkleniks*. Mork was only an average *Kerkler*, but he was still a young Orkan, and on Ork one's physical abilities get better with age.

Mindy had no intention of doing any self-*Kerkling*, though Mork looked at her expectantly. "Is it okay if I just say *Kerkle*?" she asked timidly.

"Well, it's your house. By the way, I will be staying here, won't I? I've heard so much about your Earthling hospitality."

Mindy hadn't thought about this problem. But she couldn't let him go elsewhere. He would be noticed in a minute. "Well, I guess it's okay, but I sure hope my father doesn't find out."

"You see?" Mork said. "I have learned already. A Father is a person who wears his jacket backward, correct?"

Mindy patiently began to explain, but Mork interrupted. "Is this very important?" he asked.

"Well, it would help if you knew the difference."

"But I don't need to write it in my report, do I?"

"No, I guess not."

"Ah, good," Mork said. "My nail was worn out during the walk and that instant nailer makes a terrible smell."

"So you smell," Mindy said, pleased to have found a common experience.

Mork put his finger near his underarms. "I do?" he said, embarrassed.

"You smell with your finger," Mindy said, disappointed. "Do you do everything with your finger?"

Mork stiffened. "Isn't this a bit personal? What do you do everything with?"

Mindy blushed. "I'm sorry, you didn't understand. I drink with my mouth, smell with my nose, uh, see with my eyes, and hear with my ears."

Mork shook his head in dismay. "What confusion," he said sadly. "You primitive beings lead exhausting lives."

"Primitive?" Mindy felt angry for all human beings. "What makes us primitive, because we don't drink with our fingers?"

"*Nin, nin*," Mork said, using yet another of the Orkian no's. This one was used only for philosophical discussions. "You don't understand living forms. Look how you cage the plants and you eat animals and you kill each other—"

Mindy quickly interrupted. She was made sad by this list. "Your planet doesn't do any of those things?"

"Not since two *bill-krells*."

"How do you eat?"

"We eat plant leavings."

Mindy was confused. "You eat dead leaves?"

"*Nap, nap.* We eat the colored extrusions."

"You mean flowers? You eat flowers?"

"And coffee, of course."

"But coffee and flowers don't have any nourishment," Mindy said.

Mork shook his head in disapproval. "And you say you're not a primitive life-form?"

"Amazing. Coffee and flowers. What else is different on Ork?"

"The biggest difference is that we don't allow emotions."

Mindy leaned forward. "You don't allow them, or you don't have them? Which is it?"

"Hmm." Mork put his finger up in the air. "Interesting. A little of both."

"Did Orkans ever have emotions?"

"Oh, many, many emotions." Mork moved around the room making noises. "*Raftzins, Jows,* and, worst of all, *Links*."

"And what are those emotions?" Mindy was fascinated. Perhaps they would be feelings that no human has ever had. A brand-new emotion.

"I have no idea," Mork said. "It's illegal to know."

Mindy tried to understand. "Then what's the point of having words for them?"

"Oh, we have words for many things that don't exist."

"But that's not what I mean, Mork. Do you have many words that don't mean anything at all?"

Mork was surprised. "Certainly. Don't you?"

"No, our words always mean something. Sometimes they mean different things, but they always have a meaning." Mindy began to feel nervous because Mork continued to stand. "Mork, you can sit down and make yourself comfortable."

"Ah! *Pah-poo*." Mork walked to the chair and very easily sat down on it. Everything was done easily, which was amazing because Mork had sat down on his face. Mindy stared at his legs, which were up in the air, moving gently, as if Mork were bicycling.

"Mork, what are you doing?"

"I made myself comfortable."

"You sit on your face?"

"Of course."

"Of course," Mindy mumbled to herself. This was going to be much harder than she had thought at first. Though he looked perfectly human, there was nothing Mork did that wasn't utterly different from the way humans did things.

"Mork, you can't sit like that on Earth."

"No?"

"No, and that voice!" Mindy had almost become used to Mork's speedy, high-whining voice, but every other time he spoke, she realized how strange his speech was. "Mork, can you sit the way I'm sitting?"

Mork stared at Mindy, which, since he was upside down, looked very odd. "Don't be *miltz*," he said with scorn. He quickly got up and sat normally (for a human).

"*Miltz*?" Mindy laughed. "What does that mean?"

"Nothing—the word doesn't exist," Mork lied, though, in fact, Orkans can't lie; they can only exaggerate greatly. *Miltz* had been outlawed only two *krells* ago, since its meaning, the Kant council decided, could only be used in an insulting fashion, and insults are against the law. *Miltz* used to mean what the word "silly" means in English.

Fortunately, Mindy was too concerned about Mork's voice. She had put a hand sadly to her head. "What are we going to do about your voice?"

"You don't like my voice? I'll change it." Mork lowered his head and spoke in a cowboy drawl. "If you don't get off that horse nice and slow, I'm gonna blow you off." Mork changed his voice again. "Book 'em, Dano," he said, sounding like a tough detective.

"Where did you learn those voices?"

"We've been monitoring your television for years. My favorite is that very sad program about the stranger on your planet who lives with the loud redhead."

"What's the name of that program?"

"'I Love Lucy.' Babalooo," Mork sang, in a perfect imitation. "By the way," he continued, looking gravely at Mindy, "how *is* poor little Ricky?"

Mindy shook her head. "I can see this is not going to be easy."

"Problems?" Mork tilted his head and looked

soothingly at Mindy. "Try Compoz. Many women find that occasional tension and anxiety—"

"That voice!" Mindy yelled excitedly. "That's almost normal."

"Thank you. We will return to the second half of 'Another—"

"Mork," Mindy said, "can you choose your own words and speak in that voice?"

"Of course," Mork said, his voice still deep and resonant.

"Mork," Mindy said, jumping up from the couch, excited, "we've made a breakthrough!"

Mork got up and begun to jump exactly the way Mindy was. "I think I like 'breakthroughs,'" Mork said in his Orkian voice.

Mindy pointed her finger at him. "The other voice."

But Mork didn't pay attention. Instead, he covered his face and began to curl up. "Mork!" Mindy cried out. "What's the matter?"

"Your *bloink*. I did nothing—"

Mindy stared down and realized that she was pointing her index finger at Mork. "Oh, Mork," she said, putting a hand on his arm, "it's nothing. I can't do anything with my finger."

Mork looked up, shocked. "Nothing? Nothing at all?"

"I can't do what you can do with yours. Boy, this is a silly conversation," she said to the walls.

"On my planet," Mork said, getting to his feet, "that is a very serious gesture. It is the first of our more than two *yellion* laws. Every mother teaches it to her children—never point at strangers; it's not nice."

Mindy listened only partly to him. She was busy being amazed by how Mork's arm had felt when she touched it briefly. At first it felt like stone, something very hard and strong. But within a moment of contact, his arm had become soft and yet still very firm. The whole experience was very unsettling. It brought home to her, among other things, that this was a very remarkable experience. She wondered for a moment if it was right for her to keep Mork's presence a secret. Scientists could probably learn more things in a minute talking to Mork than in a hundred years of research.

Mork waved his hand in front of Mindy. "Very strange. I wonder if all humans fall asleep so quickly."

"Oh, Mork, I'm sorry. Mork, you're still talking the wrong way."

Mork nodded and turned his head in the other direction. "Is that better?" he asked, still speaking like a fast tape recorder.

"No, no. Don't you remember? We chose that voice you learned from our television."

"Oh, yes. That was before the breakthrough. I didn't realize I had changed voices. But, you know, that's how we pay our bills around here," he said, speaking like an announcer.

"That's good, Mork. But you must use your own words while still using that voice."

"Very good, Mindy, I understand. This sounds normal for Earth?"

Mindy smiled. "Well, pretty much." She looked at the clock and exclaimed, "Oh, I must get to bed. Listen, we've made good progress. Now, you can sleep here on the couch. I'll bring you some sheets and blankets."

Mork examined the couch doubtfully, while Mindy went to the closet. "Ah," Mork said when she opened its door. "Well, Mindy," he said, sounding like FM radio, "it's not going to be so hard to fit right in here."

Mork had reached the closet and he said, "Good morning," while turning upside down, hooking his feet on the closet bar, and hanging.

"You sleep like that?" Mindy cried out hopelessly.

"Well, usually I prefer a walk-in with a window, but this will do."

And with that, Mork settled in for a good night's sleep on Earth.

* * *

5

Mindy McConnell's mother had died when Mindy was ten. Her father, Frederick, had asked Mindy's grandmother to move in with him and help raise Mindy. Frederick's friends were always amazed by that. Being willing to live with his mother-in-law for Mindy's sake proved how much he loved his daughter. Frederick had been disappointed in his career; he dreamed of being a symphony conductor, but, in fact, he owned a music store.

He had run the store for ten years, always trying to resist giving in to popular music. Cora, his mother-in-law, had to yell at him so that he would stock rock 'n' roll records. She began to learn about the music of the young to help improve their business, and soon she began to play it for her own enjoyment. By now, she was the most fanatical teeny-bopper on the block. Though that was good for business, it bothered Frederick to no end. He hated the new music as much as he adored his classical records, his beautiful pianos, violins, oboes, and all the other things that, as Cora put it, "no one would buy." Frederick was made so bitter by the buying habits of the young that he distrusted everything about them. Long hair, casual clothing, slang, and, especially, living together without getting married: all were part of the same thing to him—bad taste in music.

But he had to put up with Cora and her policy in the store. Because it was the electronic guitars, amplifiers, and Moog synthesizers, along with the modern music, that made the store profitable business. Even with those things, the store had many problems, most of them caused by its plumbing and a man named Arnold Wanker. Mr. Wanker was their landlord and he wanted to force Frederick to move out because Mr. Wanker could then double the rent. But Mindy's father had a lease that entitled him to remain for three more years, and so Mr. Wanker would let the heat go off, or keep it low, or he would have construction work going on outside so that people wouldn't want to go in the store. No, life was not easy for Frederick, but still he loved his daughter and even Cora in many ways, and he was surrounded all day by the instruments and records he loved.

Cora liked to tease Frederick about the new music and this morning had begun with her statement that Alice Cooper's music had more feeling than Beethoven's *Fifth Symphony*. When Mindy came into the store, the argument had gotten noisy.

"Alice Cooper!" Frederick yelled. "Alice Cooper just beats the keys with a dead snake!"

"At least he plays with feeling," Cora said.

Mindy groaned, "Are you two going to start this again?"

"*I,*" Frederick said, standing proudly in the middle of the store, pointing to himself, "am a musician. I sell violins, cellos—"

"You mean, you *don't* sell them," Cora mumbled.

"That is food for the spirit, a feast for the soul. While you peddle junk food."

"Frederick," Cora said, pushing her face, smooth and rosy despite her years, at him, "if you were in heaven and God said to you, 'I will give you a wish; you can be born with brains, or you can be born with a permanent rash on your fanny,' which would you choose, dear?"

This question stopped Frederick from raving. He tried to figure out what the trap was. "The brains," he said slowly.

"Good," Cora snapped. "I see you've learned by your mistake." And with that she exited triumphantly to the back room.

Fred looked unhappily at Mindy. "If it weren't for the memory of your mother— Ah, she's a foolish woman. Imagine such talk at her age."

"Dad, you know she loves you. These arguments keep her young."

Fred had paid no attention. He had been staring at Mindy's face. "You look like you haven't slept very much."

Mindy turned away. "Now, Daddy, that's not a good way to build up a girl's ego. I turn twenty-one and already you start telling me I look old."

"Not *old.* Sleepy." Fred continued to peer in her direction, even though Mindy kept her back to him. "Didn't you go out with that young man last night?"

"All *right,*" Mindy said, turning back toward her father. "I didn't get much sleep. I was up half the night talking to the most fascinating person."

"Bill? The most fascinating person?" Fred began to tap his fingers nervously against one of the pianos.

"Not Bill. Someone else."

"You were up half the night with a strange man?"

Mindy sighed hopelessly. Was there any way to stop his suspicions? "Daddy, I said *talking*." She looked angry.

Fred immediately felt foolish and smiled. "I'm sorry. I do trust you." Now he looked slyly at her. "I'm still upset about your running away from home."

"I didn't run away from home, Dad. I'm twenty-one."

Fred laughed and hugged her. "I'm teasing you. I'll always think of you as a little girl. You have to forgive me for that."

"I do," Mindy said quietly.

"So who was this fascinating man?" Fred asked, trying to sound casual.

"Well," Mindy said, "I want you to meet him. Now, he's a little unusual. He's not familiar with some of our customs—"

"Oh, God!" Fred exclaimed. "What is he? An Arab?"

"It's hard to explain, Dad. He's outside. Let me get him."

Mindy had decided that she couldn't leave Mork alone all day. So she thought, after a very difficult session of preparing Mork, that she would see what her father would make of him. At the worst, she could confide in Fred and be sure that the secret was safe. She had left Mork just around the corner, and she told him not to move. The moment she got back she realized her mistake. Three people had gathered around Mork and were

staring at him because Mork had stood completely
still while Mindy was away.

Mork couldn't understand why Mindy wanted
him to stand that way, especially when other
humans began to bump into him, yell strange
words, and then stare. Some had even begun to
laugh, but that meant he was doing something
pleasurable, so Mork didn't worry about those people—he just worried about the ones who yelled.
After a while, Mork noticed that there was another
human, in the park across the way from him, who
was also standing very still. But no one looked or
yelled or laughed at him, though the birds seemed
to enjoy sitting on his head.

Just before Mindy arrived, one of the people
who watched him began to poke Mork in the chest.
At first, he did so lightly and jumped back, as if
Mork had an electric charge. "He's as hard as a
rock," the man said.

"He's better at this than the Queen's guards,"
another person said. "I swear he hasn't blinked
once."

At this moment, Mindy arrived, terrified to dis-
cover that her careful plan had already gone amiss.
"Ha! Ha!" she said loudly. "What a kidder," Mindy
said to the onlookers.

"Ah, Mindy," Mork said in his announcer's voice,
"I don't like this ritual and I don't understand the
point of it."

"Ha! Ha!" Mindy said, taking Mork's arm and
quickly leading him away.

Mork went with her, saying, "I know that other
fellow didn't seem to mind, but I don't like to have
birds walk on my head."

Mindy didn't even want to know what Mork
was talking about. She hurried him toward the

store, whispering, "Mork, I didn't mean you had to stand *completely* still. I just meant that you shouldn't go anywhere."

"I'm afraid your earthling language is too confusing," Mork answered while they entered the music store.

Fred wasn't pleased at the sight of Mork in his casual clothes, which were overalls and a bright yellow T-shirt.

"Uh, Dad," Mindy said, "this is Mork. Mork, Mr. McConnell."

"Hello!" Mork's voice boomed. "How are you today?"

Fred shook his head, surprised by the resonance of Mork's voice.

Mork, thinking this was a part of the greeting ritual that Mindy had forgotten to tell him about, also shook his head, but harder.

"Who is this?" Fred said to Mindy. "Some hippie friend?"

"Dad, that's not very polite."

Fred looked at Mork's hand and shook it reluctantly. "Hello," he said.

"Hello!" Mork boomed.

Fred looked uncertain and said quietly, "Nice to meet you."

"Nice to meet *you!*" Mork sounded like a stereo turned all the way up. Mindy thought she could hear the walls vibrate.

"Could you speak a little lower?" Fred said.

Oh, no, Mindy thought. Sure enough, Mork bent his knees and dropped down a few inches. "Nice to meet *you,*" he said melodically.

"I don't think this is very funny, Mindy," Fred said, his face reddening. "If this punk—"

Mindy pulled Mork away toward the door. "I'll

be right back, Dad. I just want to show Mork how to get home."

"Where are you going?" Fred yelled, but Mindy and Mork were out the door, scurrying down the street.

"Is this the usual pace?" Mork asked while they ran around the corner again.

"Oh, God," Mindy said, leaning against the wall when she stopped. "I don't know what I'm going to do about you."

"Who is this God?" Mork asked.

"Oh, Mork, I can't explain about God now."

"I'm just surprised that there are invisible earthlings."

Mindy looked blank.

"You keep talking to him, but I don't see him," Mork explained.

It was then that Mindy realized that if Mork took everything she said literally, she could send him back to her apartment without a worry. "Now, listen carefully, Mork," she said.

Mork took his right index finger, cradled it in his left hand, and placed it near Mindy's mouth, though, of course, not pointing at her.

"Walk to my home the same way we walked here. Take these keys and put them in the lock and open the door and go inside and close the door behind you. Then wait until I get home, okay?"

"Yes," Mork said seriously.

"Oh," Mindy realized, "and before you close the door behind you, take the keys out."

Mork agreed and went off, unperturbed by all these adventures, since they were no stranger to him than normal events would have been. He thought Earth was an odd place. Most of the time, what humans said wasn't what they meant. But

Mork put that down to the fact that as a primitive people, they had no illegal words. Illegal words were the key to Orkian social progress. Mork decided that until that development occurred, things were probably as uncertain on Ork as they are on Earth.

* * *

6

Mork had no trouble walking home backward, making the same hand gestures he had earlier. As an Orkan, he could use his finger as a guide. Human beings certainly enjoy observing, he thought to himself as he noticed the stares and open-mouthed expressions on people's faces wherever he went.

Once he had followed Mindy's instructions on how to regain entry to her apartment, Mork decided to occupy the waiting time with a memory recall. On Ork these were referred to as *Efruds*— a trance where you relive a past experience. First he hung himself by the legs from the closet bar and then put his index finger on his nose. The room hummed. And slowly Mork's face turned pink. This was called: Remembering Through a Pink-Colored Face.

Twenty years ago (or *blems*, as an Orkan would say when speaking of Earth time) a young man named Arthur Fonzerelli was sitting in an Earth home of a family named Cunningham. He had just

answered the phone. "Yo," he said, a hand strok-
ing his greased, back-combed hair on his temples,
"Cunningham residence." He frowned. "No, Richie
is not here. He and the family are takin' a week's
vacation." The Fonz, as he is known to most Earthlings, made his voice husky. "You sound cute.
What's your name? Mary? This," he said, puffing
his chest out, "is Arthur Fonzerelli, house-sitter."

The Fonz banged the telephone down on the
table quickly and brought it back to his ear.
"What!? You never heard of me? Are you new in
town?" he said in a sly voice. "Or are you just
recently back from lunch? Yeah, I'll tell him you
called," he answered without enthusiasm. He
brushed his hair back as he hung up the phone,
looking bored. "That Richie hangs around with
real losers."

The Fonz, let it be said, was a reasonable man,
and he began to write down the message on a pad
put next to the phone for that purpose. But a whirring sound, coming from the window behind him,
brought him to a halt. A giant egg, shining white,
had lowered to the ground. By the time the Fonz had
turned to face the window, the whirring noise
had stopped. "All right," he said, leaning back on
his heels, "who's going wheee, wheee, wheee?"
The Fonz walked to the door. "Ralph," he said
loudly, "if that's you doing a bad joke, you'll find
out I don't like wheee, wheee, wheee." The Fonz
quickly opened the door, and standing there was
Mork, dressed in his red spacesuit, with a silver
square on his chest, and his head covered by a
helmet that blacked out his face. "Whoa! Whoa!
Whoa!" the Fonz yelled in a panic, backing away
from the door.

"Greetings, Fonzie," said Mork in his high,

speedy voice. "Remember me? Mork from Ork—or, as you once called me, the 'nut from outer-space-amondo.' " Mork took off his space helmet.

The Fonz, confused, but remembering vaguely, said, "Uh, yeah, I had a bad dream last night. That's it," he said, confident once again, "I'm dreaming again. No wonder that chick Mary never heard of me. This is a nightmare."

"Sorry. This is a true *beypez*. I *thribilled* your mind to make you forget. I didn't wish to strain your brain."

"Hey!" The Fonz turned sideways. "Very thoughtful. I think I want to wake up now." Fonzie slapped himself across the cheeks twice.

Mork lowered his eyebrows. "Do you often slap yourself?" Mork looked at his own hand questioningly and then slapped himself twice. "I do not find that pleasurable," he decided.

The Fonz was worried. "I think I *am* awake."

Mork put out his palm reassuringly. "Do not be afraid. I will not harm you. That would be *nin*-Orkian behavior."

"Afraid?" The Fonz put his hand on his chest and then strutted back toward the door. "Me? Afraid? Hey!" He put his hands out.

"Good. I want to be friends."

The Fonz, pretending to be bored as he put his hand on the door, said, "On the other hand, as much as I'd like to invite you in for a small talk, I'm really busy." He looked harassed. "I gotta write a note to Richie from Mary. Uh, I gotta wipe the bugs off my headlights." He began to close the door. "Important stuff."

The door was halfway closed when Mork pointed his *bloink* and made a short hum. The Fonz tried to keep closing the door, but it wouldn't budge. "But

this is important, too," Mork said. "Last time I was
here, I observed an Earth ritual that I cannot comprehend. It's been driving me *ka-bloink*."

The Fonz, still trying to push the frozen door
shut, glanced nervously at Mork. "Hey, listen. Don't
get tense, you know what I'm saying? We'll talk
about it. Uh, what's this ritual that drives you, you
know, that bothers you?"

"Men dating women," Mork answered.

The Fonz backed away and smiled. This was his
kind of talk. "I think you came to the right guy."
He lifted his chin proudly. "What do you want to
know?"

Mork pointed his finger at the door and then
bent it back at the joint. There was another hum,
and Fonz, who had been leaning against it, nearly
fell down as the door began to close. Mork walked
in and Fonz closed the door, puzzled. "Hey,
thanks," he said doubtfully.

"Why," Mork said, "does a man date a woman?"

The Fonz shook his head. "This is basic stuff. I
mean, men don't go out with women on your planet?"

Mork thought about this. Assuming he understood what this Earthling meant by men and wom-
en, he decided, "Could be. It's hard to tell. Parts
are interchangeable."

The Fonz walked to the couch and sat down. "I
don't know how you guys ever got so far advanced.
You have no incentive!"

Mork walked to the couch and sat on his face.

The Fonz was appalled. "Hey! Hey! I got problems talking to someone who sits like that."

"Sorry," Mork said, standing up and looking at
Fonzie. "I will sit Fonz-like." And Mork sat down

the human way, but so close to Fonz that their shoulders were pressed together.

"Don't touch me," Fonzie said ominously. Mork moved obediently to the other side of the couch. "Now, let me approach this scientifically. First thing to know: Have you ever kissed a girl?"

Mork turned his head to the left and then to the right, an amusing Orkian gesture of amazement. Mork had forgotten that Fonz wouldn't understand this last remaining legal bit of Orkian humor. "Kiss? I do not know what that word means, but the word has a nice ring. Kiss, kiss, kiss," Mork said, pursing his lips. When he did that, there was a slight bell sound.

Fonzie stared at him. "Oh, boy. This is truly a task only the Fonz can handle. A kiss, my friend, is when a guy and a girl put their lips together and then sort of grind them around, and around, and around."

"Ground lips?" Mork looked sad. "It sounds unappealing."

"Hey!" The Fonz was irritated. "Don't knock it until you try it."

"*Pah-poo*," Mork said, standing up and heading for the door.

"Where ya going?" Fonz yelled after him.

Mork stopped and looked surprised. "Out to grind a girl's lips."

"No, no, no," Fonzie said. He rushed to the door and began leading Mork back. "The girl has to be willing. Hey," Fonzie said, looking at Mork's arm, "your arm sure is going through a lot of changes. Anyway, you don't just grab a girl and grind her lips—I mean, kiss her. She has to"—Fonz moved his hands and his body slowly—"know you. You understand?"

"Oh. Perhaps you know a girl who's willing."

"I know 'em willing and able. And not willing, but willing to be convinced."

"Then can you introduce me to one?"

The Fonz looked at Mork with admiration. "You *are* a direct person. It's not that easy. Hey."

"But," Mork said, about to commit an Orkian crime, that of flattery, "you are known throughout the galaxy for your expertise in this matter."

"I am?" Fonzie recovered quickly. "Oh, I am, of course. It is better than having you walk around the town by yourself. Okay, I'll get you a date. But first you gotta go upstairs and put on some of Richie's clothes. I mean, you gotta look decent."

"Thank you," Mork said, walking up the stairs to Richie's room. "My suit does need pressing."

"Don't thank me. You still need a lot of work before you meet a girl. It's a good thing you got me." As soon as he was alone, Fonzie sat down at the kitchen table and tried to think of whom he could phone. "Should I get Gloria Hickey for him? Naw, I don't want to freak her out." Fonz snapped his fingers. "Hey! Maybe the Hooper triplets! Now, there's a six-pack to go. Naw, I don't want to freak *him* out." Fonzie took out his comb and began to do his hair in front of a mirror, knowing that his best thinking was always brought out by the sight of his own beauty. And, sure enough, the brainstorm was not long in coming. He made his call and then yelled for Mork to hurry and come downstairs.

Within a second, Mork came flying down the staircase, hitting the wall hard. Fonzie shouted and ran over, asking, "Are you all right?"

Mork jumped to his feet. "Was that sufficiently hurried? Is that how you humans begin the dating ritual?" He looked around and didn't understand. "Where is she? If she's here, she must be tiny."

"Hey!" The Fonz rocked back on his heels. "You have got to calm down. Wow! And we haven't even gotten to the exciting part. Now, before you meet her, there're a few things you should get straight."

Mork spread out his legs, making them rigid, and held his arms out, also straight and hard.

"What are you doing!" Fonz almost shouted.

"Getting a few things straight. I began with my legs, and then went to the arms. I would do my neck, but it cuts off *gerblink* to my finger. I would probably die."

"Hey!" Fonz said. He couldn't wait for this to be over. "Relax. I want to talk about kissing."

"I have been giving that thought. I do not know why I would want to do it."

"For pleasure. Isn't there anything you do on your planet that gives you physical pleasure?"

Mork moved away and wanted to hide behind his arms, the traditional, but outlawed, sign of embarrassment. "Just one," he whispered. "But it's against the law. I couldn't tell you."

Fonz stood back on his heel and spread his arms. "Hey! We're having a talk. A man-to . . . to-whatever, talk. So tell me."

Mork put his finger up and thought. If he wished to learn this dating ritual, he must give away this most precious of Orkian secrets. But he could clear Fonzie's mind of it later, so he said, "Okay. When a woman of Ork touches a man here"—Mork touched Fonzie's wrist—"it drives an Orkian man *ka-bloink*." Mork began to tremble at the thought.

"*Ka-bloink?*" Fonzie shook his head in disbelief. "Then what?"

Mork leaned toward Fonzie. "It has only happened to me once. I had this *ka-bloink* come over me and I couldn't control myself." Mork covered himself with his arms. "I—I became a *zoowtz* and jerked her earlobe." He uncovered himself. "I sincerely regret it."

"Hey! Listen, I would regret it, too."

There was a knock on the door. "Don't move," Fonz said, and, of course, Mork froze. Fonzie rushed to the door, opened it, and grabbed the young woman standing there. She was an Earthling named Laverne. Fonzie kissed her passionately. "Give me two minutes. He's not ready yet."

Laverne's eyes swooned with pleasure. "For you, Fonzie, I'd give up milk and Pepsi forever."

"Hey! That's beautiful." Fonz slammed the door and rushed back to Mork. "Listen, if you want to get along with women, you gotta say nice things. You gotta flatter them."

"I can do that," Mork answered.

"And if it gets to where you don't know what to do, just do what Laverne does. She's been around and knows the ropes."

Mork nodded with understanding. "Oh, I know the ropes, too. I can tie a square knot, a half-hitch, a sheepshank—"

"Hey, you're not trying to get a merit badge here."

The front door opened and Laverne strolled in, trying to seem sexy. "Fonz, you said two minutes." Laverne batted her eyes at Mork. "So, you must be Morky. Pleased to meet ya. I'm Laverne." She put out her hand, tilted in Mork's direction, for him to kiss, in the European fashion.

Mork parted his fingers into units of two and scissored Laverne's hand, in the traditional Orkian handshake. "*Na-No, Na-No.* I, too, am pleased."

Laverne showed her prominent front teeth in a weak smile. "Uh-huh, nice." She quickly turned her head toward the Fonz. *"Na-No, Na-No?"*

"Well," Fonzie said in a loud voice, "I must be going." He began to make his retreat. "Two's company, three's a crowd."

Mork nodded his head vigorously, impressed. "That's very good. May I quote you?"

Laverne's eyes widened as she listened to Mork. Laverne began to trail after Fonzie, her voice worried. "Fonz, did you stick me with another jerk?"

"Jerk?" Mork repeated, and he began to violently go up and down, his arms yanking invisible ropes, his body bending almost in half at the waist. He stopped just as quickly as he had begun and looked at the staring Fonz and Laverne. "How was that?"

Laverne smiled patiently. "Fine," she said in a babyish voice to humor Mork. "Very good jerk. Fonz!" she cried out, reaching for him.

Fonzie grabbed her hand and began to return it to her. "Look," he whispered, "he's a foreigner and not used to the way we do things. Give him a chance."

Laverne always believed everything Fonzie told her, so she was reassured. "Okay," she said and looked doubtfully at Mork. "But tell him not to jerk anymore. It makes me nervous."

Fonzie nodded. "You got it." He called out to Mork. "Don't jerk anymore. I'm gonna split-amondo. I'll be up in my room, so if you need anything, just yell." Fonz took one last look at Mork, and, shaking his head, mumbled, "A square knot. Wow!" Fonzie quickly turned and went up the stairs. Laverne sadly watched him go. And then she looked back at Mork.

"Soo," she said, casually strolling in Mork's direction, "you're Mork."

"From Ork," he said.

"Uh, I'm not the greatest with geography. But isn't Ork just off of Greece?"

"*Bin, bin,*" Mork said, the informational no. "Ork has been off grease for three *bleems*. For lubricants we use *fif, seve,* or the ever-popular *limakook.*"

Laverne decided he was crazy. She nodded stupidly at him. "Isn't that nice?" she said. "I never have understood why we don't use *limakook.*"

"Your engines could not handle it. They'd blow up and pollute the air, or destroy the galaxy."

Laverne watched him carefully as she edged her way toward the couch. "That's a good reason," she said. Maybe he's kidding, she told herself, trying to cheer up.

Mork looked carefully at Laverne to find an item about which he could flatter her. Because it was a date arranged by Fonzie, Laverne had gone all out and had bought a flower for her hair. Mork chose that. "I shall flatter you now."

"Oh, yeah?"

"You have a pretty fungus growing out of your hair."

Laverne began to thank him. "Oh, you sweet talker, you." And then she realized what Mork had said. "A fungus?"

These Earthlings understand so little of science, Mork thought. Well, he would teach her. "Fungus: any of a major group of fungi, including mushrooms and *jequts,* molds and mildew."

He was a cut-up, Laverne decided. "Oh, yeah," she answered to give him back a taste of his sarcasm. "I always wear mildew when I want to impress a guy."

Mork nodded. This flattery ritual seemed boring. "I'm impressed," he said, giving it one last fling. "Is it time to kiss yet?" Mork leaned toward her and began to move his lips one way and then the other, sliding them back and forth.

Laverne watched him with disgust. "Uh, I don't think so."

"Sorry. I am new to this dating ritual. What is the next step?"

Laverne was beginning to be charmed by his frank admission of ignorance. "Well?" she said uncertainly, moving toward the couch. "Why don't we sit down?"

Laverne sat down and began to arrange herself when she noticed that Mork had sat down with his head in the couch. "Oh!" she said, moving away. "Would ya look at that!"

Mork got to his feet. "*Fax?*" Mork said, looking around. When an Orkan looks alarmed, as Laverne did, it is usually because a *fax* has flown into the room. A *fax* is a green insect that bites, like our mosquito, only the itching welt doesn't appear until another month passes. When he noticed nothing was there, he said, "Look at what?"

Laverne relaxed. "Never mind. It's gone now."

Mork looked at her. "You also sit Fonz-like. Ah, must copy and adjust." Mork sat down normally, but right next to Laverne, his body touching hers all along one side.

Boy, he learns fast, she thought, pushing him away and moving to one end of the couch. Mork, remembering Fonzie's advice, copied her. He moved to the other end. Laverne crossed her legs, and so did Mork. She pulled her skirt down to cover her knees, and Mork pulled at his pants legs. She fluffed her hair and Mork did the same. Laverne still hadn't noticed. But when she turned her head at him and put her arm along the side of the couch, she noticed he was in the same posture. She smiled uncertainly. Mork also flashed his teeth at her. She frowned and so did he.

"Your move," he said.

"Are you making fun of me?" Laverne yelled, putting her hands on her hips, half-rising. "I don't like it when guys make fun of me. I'll give you a fat lip." Laverne made her hand into a fist and shook it threateningly.

"Oh, oh," Mork said. "Rejection. Return to hatching state!" And he curled up, putting his *bloink* in his mouth.

Laverne was moved by this pathetic sight. "Hey, it's okay. I didn't mean to reject you. It's okay," she said, moving over to his side.

Mork still stayed all cuddled up, moaning. "I just wanted to experience the dating process and make friends," he said pathetically. On Ork, however, his behavior is considered more like our anger. It is as violent as they get.

It made Laverne feel mean. "Aw. I know how you feel. You're a stranger and I should consider that. Hey." She reached for him and her hand touched his wrist. "I want to be your friend."

Mork's legs shot out and his hair puffed. "*Zeep, zeep, zeep, zeep,*" he began to say, his head bobbing each time. Laverne recoiled. "*Guzoom, guzoom, guzoom,*" Mork went, slowing down.

"What happened?"

"You touched me. Relate, relate, relate. In control, in control." Mork's head continued to twitch.

"I don't understand," Laverne said, reaching for

his wrist again, but this time with all her fingers. "All I did was this." And she took a firm hold.

"A *gang neb!*" Mork screamed. His arms flung outward and he jumped to his feet. *"Neb-zeep, Neb-zeep."* He was standing in the middle of the room now, his head jerking. "I'm in control. *Gang-neb!*" he screamed again, losing control. "Give me your earlobe," he said, turning on Laverne, his eyes shining.

Laverne crawled off of the couch, trying to get to her feet and keep an eye on Mork. "What?" she mumbled, panicked. She had known guys who were starved for affection, but this was ridiculous.

"Your earlobe!" Mork said with significance, as if he had just named the most prized possession in the universe. "Your delicious, pert earlobe!"

Laverne began to run around the sofa, keeping it between herself and Mork. But he pointed his *bloink* and the couch slid to one side, clearing his path. Laverne's eyes widened and she made a run for the stairs, but Mork caught up to her, his hand in the Orkian handshake position, ready to clutch her wonderful earlobe.

Laverne had no choice. She had to resort to her ultimate weapon against crazed blind dates. She kicked him in the shins.

Mork had no reaction. Orkans have no nerves. But he thought Laverne's action was part of the Earthling dating ritual, and he wanted her earlobe so badly that he immediately kicked her in the shins, hoping that would please her.

"Ow!" Laverne said, her hand reaching for the hurt spot. "I think we're getting off on the wrong foot."

Mork had also grabbed his leg and begun hopping, in imitation. "Oh," he said, embarrassed that he had followed directions badly. Using his other foot, he kicked her in the other shin. "Now, give me your earlobe," he said, tired of all this flattery.

Laverne screamed as Mork's fingers got hold of her earlobe and he trembled, saying, *"Nep-zizzam!"* his hair blossoming into a cloud.

"Fonz!" Laverne yelled. "Help me! Help me! He wants my earlobe!"

* * *

7

Mindy had spent all day trying to explain Mork's behavior to her father. Fred complained that as soon as she had left home, she had begun to hang around with hippies and deadbeats. He had asked her earlier what Mork did for a living, and Mindy had made the mistake of saying that he didn't have a job. She was worried whether or not Mork had really followed her directions. She phoned after lunch, but there was no answer. She couldn't remember if she had told him to sit still in the apartment, because if she had, then of course he wouldn't answer the phone. Then she worried about a fire or some other disaster occurring with Mork sitting motionless through the catastrophe. Maybe Orkans couldn't burn, she told herself to cheer up. And, in fact, they don't. They were fireproofed many *bleams* ago. But they could smoulder to death if their automatic sprinkler doesn't work. They have water systems in both pinkies that are replenished whenever they drink with their *bloink*.

Fred made an attempt to convince Mindy to have dinner with him. He asked her because he thought he might find out more about this suspicious new boyfriend. Mindy, anxious to get home, refused too quickly and firmly to calm Fred. And after she rushed off to go home, he debated with himself for some time over just how nosy it would be if he dropped in on Mindy unannounced.

When Mindy got to her apartment, she was surprised to find that Mork was moving around—not only moving around, but talking. He was standing near the phone, watching it carefully, and saying, "*Grenzel?*"

"Mork, hello."

"Greetings."

"Why are you talking to the phone?"

"I think your radio is not functioning," Mork said. "It plays only one tune."

"Mork, that's not a radio. It's a telephone."

"Ah, your primitive communication device that is your mother figure. But how did you get hold of one of Ork's hit songs?"

"I don't understand, Mork."

Mork picked up the receiver and held it out. All Mindy heard was the dialtone. Mork began to snap his fingers. "The instrumental to *Grenzel*. Very big hit."

Mindy took off her coat and sighed. Mork looked at her with concern. "I have caused heavy sigh," he said, sighing heavily. "Why is that?"

Mindy began to pace. "Mork, you are so far away from passing for an Earth—I mean a human being, that I don't know what to do."

"Perhaps you should accompany me for the next few days until I become accustomed to your world."

"I can't do that, Mork," Mindy said, her voice strained. "I have to go to work every day, except for Sunday."

"Work? What is work?"

"You know, a job. To earn money."

"You mean you have to work to make money?"

"Of course."

Mork put his finger in the air. "What a novel concept. Does everyone work?"

"Well, almost everyone."

"Who doesn't work?"

"Well, let's see. Children, uh, students—"

"What are students?"

"Students are young people who study. You know, they learn things."

"Your old people do not learn anything?"

Mindy thought of her father. "Some of them don't. I don't understand, Mork. Don't you have to work?"

"No. On Ork the only reason to work is to see the universe."

"Well, I'm afraid this brings up another problem—which is, how are you going to make money?"

"Mindy, I am from a highly advanced race. Do you think my superiors would send me to this planet without money?" Mork opened the closet and rummaged around inside until he found a sack. The bag he brought out was enormous and Mindy's eyes lit up.

"Wow! All that is money?" she asked.

"Of course," Mork said. He plunked the sack down in front of her and opened it.

Mindy peered inside, looked puzzled, and then reached in, digging.

"Careful, you're spilling," Mork said as grains of sand fell on the floor.

"Mork, this is just sand."

Mork barked his strange laugh. "Ha! Ha! You Earthlings consider nothing above humor. That is merely part of my family fortune."

"Mork, on Earth, sand is as common as dirt."

Mork stared down at his sack. "You mean this is nothing here? It is not worth more than a broken *hockle*?"

Mindy answered quietly. "I'm afraid not."

"Well, what do you use as money on this planet?"

Mindy began to explain, but she thought better of it and reached for her purse. "You caught me on a good day," she said, pulling out a five-dollar bill. "I actually have some."

Mork stared at the bill and then ran his finger over it. "But this is nothing more than paper and ink."

"Well, this is nothing more than sand," Mindy answered.

Mork put his finger in the air. "Ah, but paper and ink are common on Ork. I can obtain—"

"No, no, no, Mork. There is plenty of paper and ink on Earth. But only the government has the right to print it into money."

Mork thought about that. "But this green paper has no value of its own?"

"Well, but it is backed by things that are rare and valuable."

"What prevents other Earthlings from making their own green paper?"

"It's against the law."

This impressed Mork. The law, as has been said many times, is Ork's most precious possession.

Every citizen on Ork is a trained lawyer. That is necessary because otherwise it would be impossible to talk. An Orkan ignorant of the law would be thrown into jail as soon as he tried to speak. For example, of the six different Orkian hellos, four of them, if said to the wrong person, can get you one-to-two *krell* on the spider farm.

"Well," Mork said, "I have already learned many things. One, this phony voice." He meant his announcer's deep tones.

"Oh, Mork, I meant to tell you that you must speak just a little bit softer. I mean, lower the volume a bit."

"Two," Mork went on, his voice now lower, "don't drink with my finger. And, three, don't sit on my face."

As they talked, Fred had slowly opened Mindy's front door, and by now he was listening to their conversation. He was about to say hello when Mindy said, "You forgot the fourth thing, and it's most important. Don't tell my father that we are living together."

"I don't understand. He doesn't want you living?"

Fred's eyes got large and he felt terrible hearing his daughter conspire to fool him.

"It's not the living he wouldn't understand. It's the *together*."

"No, I wouldn't!" Fred yelled, walking into the room. He had not been so upset since his wife had died. He felt betrayed and his whole life suddenly seemed wrong and unhappy. He looked at Mindy and couldn't be sure he knew who she really was.

"Dad!" Mindy said, her heart leaping into her mouth. What had he heard? she wondered with fear.

"Greetings, Mr. McConnell," Mork said cheerfully. He was glad to see more of other Earthlings. Orson would be pleased by his thoroughness.

Fred glared at this silly hippie and wished he could think him away. "Don't 'greetings' me, you!" He looked at his daughter, who was blushing and unable to meet her father's eyes. "I wanted to believe you today." He put his arms out. "And I came here hoping I wouldn't find—" Fred was so upset, he couldn't even say "living together." "What I've found," was the only way he could refer to it.

"You came here to check on me?" Mindy asked, outraged by her father's lack of trust, even though she had lied to him.

"I came here to see my daughter—because I love her and I wanted to be sure that she wasn't getting involved with the wrong people. And, instead, I find out that she has been lying to me and that she is not only involved with a wiseacre hippie who has no job, but she is living with him."

Mindy was torn between the desire to tell her father that he had no right to talk that way and the desire to explain the truth about Mork. "Dad, it's not that way," she began.

But Fred, tears beginning to fill his eyes, kept talking, "I can't bear to think of how your mother would feel about this. I have failed her. I had only one task, to raise you to be as good and true as she was, and I couldn't." Fred looked once more at Mindy and then he quickly turned and left.

Mork walked to the door as it closed behind Fred and said cheerfully, his voice resonant and deep, "Good-bye. Thanks so much for dropping by."

Mindy couldn't bear it. "Oh, Mork, stop it!" she said, unable to stop herself from crying. She couldn't bear to look at Mork, standing stiffly, looking puzzled. She went into her bedroom to cry it out alone.

Mork thought for a moment and then took out his pad and wrote down: "Must ask why humans water their faces, and what this has to do with parenthood."

**

8

Fred walked home blindly. Though he dreamed occasionally of conducting an orchestra, he had no serious expectation that he ever would. Mindy, for almost twenty years, had been all he lived for. She had given him a few little disappointments. For one, she had never taken music as seriously as he would have liked. She didn't keep up her piano lessons. But she had been an excellent, hard-working student. And, most of all, she had grown up to be a beautiful, tall young woman, always polite and considerate. When Fred would hear other parents complaining about their children, it was with great pride that he could think of Mindy and her virtues. But now all that was gone. In a minute of conversation, Fred had heard her confess that she had lied to him, and she was conspiring to keep up the lie with this ridiculous young man. But, worst of all, she was living with him. Even if Mork had been the sort of man Fred wanted for Mindy, to live with him unmarried was a dreadful thing. It would have broken Mindy's mother's heart, and it had broken his.

He couldn't face Cora at home. She would probably make things worse by saying that Fred's feelings were foolish. Cora approved of young people living together, and she also would probably see nothing wrong with Mork's loud clothes and bizarre humor. No, he would go to the store. There, since 1967, he had kept an expensive bottle of champagne to drink when Mindy announced her engagement. But after tonight, such an announcement, if it ever came, would mean nothing. And, obviously, everything about her must be different from what he imagined, if Mork was the sort of man she loved.

At the store, he opened the champagne, thinking bitterly of all the happy moments he had raising Mindy: the first time he taught her the scale on the piano; the first day he let her work in the store. Fred stood on his side of the store drinking the champagne and looking at Cora's section. There were all the nutty electronic instruments that all sounded the same, all those horrible albums that sold like candles in a blackout. He kept drinking the champagne, hardly tasting it, though when he bought it he had thought pleasantly of how delicious each drop would be.

It was just at that moment when Deputy Sheriff Tilwick, an old friend of Fred's, walked by and noticed the lights were on. He tried the door and opened it cautiously. But when he walked in, all he saw was Fred, quite drunk, staring unhappily at his glass. "Fred?" he asked cautiously, his eyes searching for a robber. "Are you okay?"

Fred looked up stupidly. He was so drunk and miserable that even the sight of Tilwick, dressed in his well-ironed brown uniform, was unrecognizable. "Huh?"

"I saw the light on. You were supposed to be closed hours ago."

"Tilwick!" Fred said, suddenly excited as he realized who it was. He stood up and wobbled. "My old friend, it's good to see you. Come in and help me celebrate."

Tilwick smiled, relieved to hear that Fred's condition was due to a good event. Mork would have thought it strange that misery and celebration could seem so similar. Tilwick relaxed and walked eagerly over to Fred's counter, looking greedily at the bottle of champagne.

Fred picked it up and waved it around. "I have been saving this bottle for eleven years for my daughter's wedding." Fred weaved on his feet and Tilwick put out a hand to steady him. "I was reading a magazine and I heard that the Pakistanis arrange marriages between children when they are as young as eight or nine. So, I said to myself, I'm going to buy the champagne for the day when Mindy finds a young man who is as wonderful as she. In that way, I'd be a little like a Pakistani."

Tilwick reached for the bottle as Fred waved it near him, but he got only air, because Fred had waved it away again.

"Oh, her wedding!" Fred said with a silly smile. "I wanted it to be so special. Tuxedoes, flowers, a small orchestra that I would conduct. Really classy, you know?" Fred peered at the counter for another glass, but he was too drunk to see one. "Here," he said, pushing the bottle into Tilwick's chest, "you'll have to drink out of the bottle."

Tilwick laughed. The young man must be something special, he thought, for Fred to get this bombed. He took the bottle and it felt light. He swirled it around and heard nothing. Then he peered inside. "It's empty!"

Fred waved his hand. "Then suck the cork," he said and giggled hysterically at his own joke.

Tilwick decided that Fred's behavior was a little too wild to be happiness. "Fred, is everything all right?"

Fred pointed his glass at the ceiling. "A toast to the good old days," he said, then clinked his glass against the bottle. "When values were values and morals were morals. When shacking up meant building a hut."

"What are you talking about?" Tilwick said.

Fred's face fell and he leaned on the counter, staring grimly. "My daughter is living with a man."

Tilwick frowned and shook his head. He tried to picture Mindy throwing herself at some young punk. "Mindy? Naw, that can't be."

"It's true," Fred said. He was slurring his words so badly that "true" sounded like "shrew." "I heard her say it myself. I heard her," he said, trying to bang the table, but almost losing his balance instead, "tell the slob not to let me know."

Tilwick had a daughter Mindy's age; in fact, the two had gone to school together and were friends. He had always envied Fred's daughter a bit. She was always a little better at everything than his daughter. But it gave him no pleasure to hear that Mindy had fallen so low. It meant his daughter might fall even lower. "I can't believe it," he said, putting the bottle to his lips, forgetting that nothing was in it.

"I've done my best," Fred said. "It wasn't enough. But it was the best I could do."

"That's not the Mindy I know," Tilwick said.

"The way things are today," Fred said, "no matter how good a father you are, it doesn't help. Nothing can be done."

"*I* can do something!" Tilwick firmly put the bottle down on the counter.

Fred, still weaving, stared at his friend, puzzled. "What?"

"I'm a cop. I represent law and order."

Fred frowned at him. He grunted. "The boy hasn't done anything illegal, though his head should be chopped off."

Tilwick grabbed Fred's arm. "Yeah, but I can go over there and scare the daylights out of him. You know: 'Hit the road, you hamburger'—that sort of thing."

Fred hung onto his friend, his eyes shining with gratitude. "You would really do that for me?"

Tilwick patted him on the shoulder. "Tomorrow morning when I'm off duty."

Fred threw his arms around Tilwick. "*Really?*" he asked in a pathetic voice, like a starved creature who has been promised food.

Tilwick patted Fred on the back. Poor man, he thought. That boy's head *should* be chopped off. "Don't worry, Fred. I'll scare that boy so badly he'll wish he were on another planet."

* * *

9

Back at Mindy's, Mork had waited patiently until she came out of her bedroom. She had cried for a long while, both out of guilt and anger. Her father hadn't trusted her, and that made her lie to him. There didn't seem to be a way that she could behave so that Fred would approve of her. She had done none of the things he accused her of, not really. After blowing her nose, she called home to talk it out, but Fred wasn't there. Mindy didn't feel like hearing Cora insult Fred, so she didn't confide in her. There were so many problems, and Mork was the cause of all of them. It was bad enough that she didn't know where he could stay, or how he was going to make money, but now she had to figure out whether or not to confide in her father. Fred had acted so wildly that Mindy worried what he would do if she told him who Mork really was. If Fred couldn't stand her living with a hippie, how would he feel about her living with a spaceman?

Why had this happened to her? Moving out of her father's home had taken months of talking

and reassuring. Mindy still believed that Fred
wouldn't have let her move if the apartment she
found hadn't been in such a quiet, lovely old house.
Fred loved old houses as much as he liked old
music, one might say.

When Mindy finally returned to the living room,
she found Mork watching television. He was sitting
upside down, on his face, looking between his legs.

"Mork!" she yelled, shocked that he had already
forgotten.

Mork was laughing his duck laugh, and he kept
it up in spite of Mindy's order.

"Mork, I thought we agreed that you wouldn't
sit like that."

"Oh, oh," he said, leaping to his feet by jumping
clear over the back of the couch. "I am contrite."
Mork pointed to the television and it turned off.
"Ha! Ha!" he said. "A pie in the face. How original.
How unique. How do you Earthlings think of such
things?"

Mindy mumbled to herself, "My life is crazy."
And then she said aloud to Mork, "I don't think we
should go out for dinner. So I thought I would just
make some spaghetti." She looked at Mork and
saw that he had no reaction. "I hope you like
spaghetti."

"Why wouldn't I? Just because I'm from another
planet doesn't mean I'm that different."

"You just say that," Mindy answered, "because
you've been watching 'The Gong Show.' " She began
to laugh at her own joke, but Mork nodded.

"Quite true," he said. "I was going to ask Orson
if there are any other Orkans down here. From that
show, it seemed there might be several."

Mindy began to boil water. "Wait till you see
'Saturday Night Live.' " Mindy laughed again, es-

pecially when she saw Mork making a note to himself to watch it. "Mork, why don't you set the
table?"

Before Mindy could explain, Mork pointed his
bloink at the old oak table and lifted it several
feet in the air. "Where do you want me to put it?"

"That's okay. It's amazing when you do that.
Just set it down."

The table fell to the floor with a bang.

"Tomorrow is going to be a big day. We're going
to find you a place to live."

"Why can't I go on living here with you?"

Mindy sighed and so did Mork. She began to
laugh again. That was one good thing she could
say about Mork—he made every little event exciting. "Because my father is puritanical, conserva-
tive, prudish—uh, oh, what's the word I'm looking
for?"

"Your primitive language is so inexact. And it
sounds so foolish. He is a *nimnul*."

"That's it. How did you know?"

"*Nimnuls* are very common throughout the universe."

"Yes," Mindy admitted. "They are very common
here on Earth. Do you have many on Ork?"

"*Bin, bin*, we have *nuls* and *guls*, but we haven't
had a recorded case of a true *nimnul* in many
bleams. We eliminated the need for them when we
began breeding clones."

"Clones?" Mindy was fascinated. "You mean, an
exact copy of another Orkan?"

"*Yek*," Mork said, using one of the Orkian yeses.
This was for evenings only. "Oh, nothing is as
nimnul as a clone. Do you know how many clones
it takes to close an egg?" Mork asked, shaking his

head with disappointment. "One uses his *bloink* and the other two wiggle it up and down."

Mindy laughed uproariously and Mork became alarmed. "You mean you tell clone jokes on Ork?" she said, still laughing.

Mork began to look around the room and whispered frantically, "*Biz-but, biz-but.* That was not a joke, Mindy-Earthling. I could be in much trouble if Orson thought I had told a joke."

Mindy saw that Mork was serious and she covered her mouth. "I'm sorry. I thought you meant it as a joke."

"Impossible for an Orkan to mean something different from what he says. I was merely describing how *nimnul* clones are."

"Well," Mindy said, "I'm afraid that my *nimnul* is going to force us to find somewhere else for you to sleep."

Mork went to the window and pointed outside. "I saw a nice perching object right outside," he said, meaning the big maple right outside Mindy's apartment. "I could hang out there tonight."

"Wouldn't you get cold?" Mindy asked.

"No. I had my shots before I came here."

Mindy began to laugh again, but when Mork's eyes widened with fear, she stopped. "Why are you worried that this Orson, if he is a person, can hear what's happening? Isn't he on Ork?"

"Mindy," Mork said with what would have been scorn if Mork were human, "it is nothing for my superior Orson to overhear what goes on when he is a mere sixty billion light-years from a place. It's our ability to do that that made it possible for me to arrive here so well prepared."

"Mork," Mindy said, now adding the spaghetti to the boiling water, "I don't think you came here too well prepared. I admit it is your first visit, and I suppose you're no worse prepared than Columbus was."

"I do not know who this Columbus is, but I was on your planet before."

Mindy was disappointed at first to learn that she wasn't the first human to have met an Orkan. But she realized, while listening to Mork's account of his visit with the Fonz and Laverne, that they had been unable to deal with Mork as well as she had. That cheered her up considerably because up until then she thought she had made a mess of it.

She served the spaghetti and canned meat sauce with an apology: "I'm sorry that this is going to be your first Earth dinner. It's not exactly the best food to eat on our planet."

Mork stared at the white-and-red mass. "You mean, I am to ingest this?"

"Oh, that's right, I was so upset, I forgot. You eat only coffee and flowers, right?"

"*Yek*, but I can adjust." Mork pointed his index finger at his stomach and a hum began to fill the room. Mindy noticed that Mork's stomach began to glow, pulsating white and red. He snapped his fingers and it halted.

"It's okay now?" Mindy asked. "Can you also have some wine?" she said, pouring a glassful for him.

"What do you do with that?" Mork asked.

"You have it with your dinner."

"Ah." Mork rubbed his hands excitedly and poured the wine into his spaghetti. "Didn't improve it much," he said, sticking his finger in and draining the bowl of liquid in a few seconds.

"Mork," Mindy said, not knowing which mistake to discuss first, "I thought we agreed you weren't going to drink with your finger anymore."

Mork covered his finger. "Shame. Embarrassment. I will eat with my mouth and drink, too." Mork pointed at the bowl and the spaghetti unraveled into long strands that smoothly shot into Mork's mouth. Mindy watched in amazement as the whole bowl kept going steadily into Mork's mouth. He had no reaction to the continuous flow of food. He was finished in no time.

"Would you like more?" Mindy asked.

"*Yek*," Mork said.

"Oh, boy, the way you eat, we really are going to have to find you a job quickly."

"A job?" Mork said. "But I have a job. I am to report to Orson about Earth."

"But Mork," Mindy said, while she gave him more food, "you have to have a job that makes you some Earth money—you know, the green paper."

"Heavy sigh," Mork said, and then he sighed heavily. "I have to find a place to live. And then I have to find a job. You primitive life-forms are very harassed."

Mindy, as she carefully explained to Mork that he mustn't eat by making his finger transport food into his mouth, and thinking in the back of her mind about her fight with Fred, had to agree with Mork's observation. Life had become very harassed.

But Mork did have his advantages, Mindy learned when she began to wash the dishes. Mork watched her for only a few seconds before he began to bark, "Ha! Ha! Ha!"

Mindy, her hands soapy, turned to look at him.

"What wit!" Mork said and barked again. "Ha! Ha!"

"Mork," Mindy protested, "this is not a joke. I'm cleaning the dishes."

Mork covered his mouth in embarrassment. "Profound apologies. On the television entertainment device, there was a brief show about a youth serum in just such a container. I thought you were performing a satire." Mork posed like an actor. "Keep your hands young and beautiful."

"Mork, what you saw was a commercial for this." Mindy held up her bottle of dishwashing liquid. "It helps clean the dishes."

Mork was amazed. These poor Earthlings were living almost completely without technology. "Mindy," he said, "I cannot bear to see you humbled in this manner. Not since the fifth *krell* have any Orkans slaved as you slave. Step away from the sink."

Mindy knew enough by now to do as Mork said. She shut off the water, leaving the sink piled with dishes. Mork pointed his *bloink*, the tap turned, and steam began to rise, its fog obscuring one entire side of the kitchen. Mindy heard plates rattle and then saw flickers of color fly through the air. Soon, soapy bubbles also joined the steam. Mork kept his finger on the entire operation, but otherwise looked bored. In less than a minute, the water shut off and the fog cleared to reveal clean dishes neatly stacked next to the empty sink.

"Is that satisfactory?" Mork asked, without any pride in his achievement. He had none not only because Orkans are incapable of feeling pride, but also because his ability was common on Ork.

Mindy smiled at the sight. Having Mork around was like living with the greatest magician ever. Even better. "Remind me to take you to the people at Whirlpool," she said jokingly.

Mork nodded, took out his pad, and asked, "On what day should I remind you?"

"Never mind," Mindy said, realizing she couldn't joke around Mork. He took everything literally.

Mork had not used the dish drainer next to the sink, and Mindy, seeing this, said, "Uh, Mork, could you put the clean dishes into that object next to the sink?"

He nodded, pointed his *bloink,* and, one by one, the dishes, silverware, and glasses all hoisted themselves into the drainer.

"Very nice," Mindy said, delighted. She felt like a kid at the circus sideshow. "Well, I'm exhausted from having spent all last night up talking."

"I, too, am suffering from *egg-lag,*" Mork said. "On my planet right now, it's twenty-million years ago."

"Well, then we'd better both go to bed."

Mork nodded and began walking toward the closet. "Yes, I'm ready to hit the old coatrack."

"Mork," Mindy said, despairing once more of ever getting him to behave normally, by which she meant humanly, "You're on Earth now. You should sleep in a bed."

"Is that where you sleep?"

"Yes. Boy, there's a lot you have to learn."

"Good. I will sleep with you. I'm always willing to learn. It is an Orkian principle to never look a learning text in the binding."

"Uh, I think maybe it would be better if you slept on the sofa."

Mork looked down at the sofa. He remembered Mindy making it up the night before. Perhaps, he thought, amazed by the idea, Earthlings actually do sleep flat, like on the television programs. Until meeting Mindy, Mork had thought television was a fantasy world that had little to do with real life. Apparently it was grimly realistic. "Flat?" he asked. "Won't I get dizzy?"

Mindy went to the closet and got out a blanket and sheets. She wasn't sure, but while in there she thought Mork's egg luggage had moved just before she turned the light on. "Well," she said in answer to his question, "you won't have far to fall." He would need the comforter, Mindy realized, so she asked him to go up to the attic to get it, because she hated going up there.

Right next to the front door was a narrow staircase leading to a low-ceilinged attic. Mork went up there with considerably less disgust than a human would. The attic was too low to stand in. It was dark, piled with odd-shaped objects, the rafters full of spiders' webs, the whole place giving off the feeling that something awful might be hiding there.

To Mork, however, the place was pleasant, warm, cozy, just like home. And that was because Ork was just like Mindy's attic. Or pretty close. Spiders are like houseplants here on Earth, and because all of Ork's six suns are quite far away from the planet, it is very dark there. Also, dust is considered a mark of tradition, since it shows that an Orkan's possessions have been around for a long time. Also, it is considered amusing there to slide across especially dusty floors.

Mork was quite happy rummaging around up there, trying to decide which object was the comforter Mindy wanted. Finally, he decided it had to be one of two objects and he brought them both downstairs.

Mindy watched him and thought to herself:

When am I ever going to learn to be specific with him?

Mork had carried down a huge moose head and an antique car horn. He hugged the moose head. "I hope this is the comforter."

"No," Mindy said. "My comforter doesn't stare. Never mind. I'll get it later."

"Your attic," Mork said, his eyes showing admiration, "is real *kookla*." *Kookla* is a slang word that is currently under review by the Kant Council. The question is whether a word that in English would mean "groovy" is emotional or not. It has in its favor that it can be used as a compliment, and that makes it a close decision for the Council. Mork, as you can judge, was using the word very safely. He was making a sincere attempt to amend the mistakes that had gotten him exiled to Earth.

"*Kookla*?"

"Nice," Mork explained. "Dark, dusty, full of spiders. Also, I love studio apartments. They're so cozy."

"That's pleasant to you?"

"My kind of town. It's perfect. I could live there happily."

"Mork, people don't live in attics. Attics are storage spaces where you put things that are cluttering up your life."

Mork, without any self-pity, said, "You mean, like this comforter and me?" He hugged the moose head and looked openly with his clear blue eyes at her.

Of course, Mork had not meant this as an emotional plea, but it felt like one to Mindy. She felt so bad for Mork. "You're not cluttering up my life," she said sweetly. She thought about Mork's suggestion. Everything was crazy with him, so the attic probably would be a good home for him. She certainly didn't need the space, and it would solve the problem of finding him a place to live. She had been thinking all night how hard it was going to be to rent a place for him. Mork was nowhere near ready to deal with landlords. And how would he pay the rent? She couldn't afford to pay it for him, and what with inflation, most people wouldn't be satisfied with a sack of sand instead of a rent check.

"You know, Mork," she said, coming to a decision, "actually, the attic wouldn't be a bad place if we fixed it up. And it is *almost* like having your own apartment. It's a great place for you to stay while you're adjusting to Earth. It's perfect." Mindy was nearly carried away by this speech, but then she remembered her father. "Except for my father."

Mork looked innocently at Mindy. "Will he cause a big problem?"

"No, no," Mindy said. "He's really a very sweet man. He would never do anything drastic or harmful. I'll talk to him tomorrow."

✳✳✳
10

Mork had not had an easy time sleeping on the couch. Mindy wouldn't allow him to sleep in the attic that night. She kept insisting that it had to be vacuumed. When Mork inquired as to the meaning of the word, she explained that it was a device used to suck up dirt. Mork was horrified at the thought of all those lovely spiders being sucked to death, their little bodies pulled into pieces. That thought kept him awake for a time, and then trying to sleep flat was a terrible trial.

He put his hand on the floor to maintain his balance, but by the morning his head was on the ground and his feet had hooked onto the backrest, and he was as upside down as he would have been in the closet.

Mindy, when she saw how scrunched up and funny his face looked, decided not to complain that he had reverted to Orkian habits. She hurried through breakfast, making a pot of coffee for Mork, which he drank (with his mouth) in gulps. He looked much happier afterward and Mindy promised to bring him some flowers for lunch. She planned to tell her father the truth and bring him home to prove that Mork was really from Outer Space.

She told him to stay inside, and he, of course, obeyed. Soon after she left, he opened the refrigerator to learn more about this food depository. What he saw inside astonished and terrified him. He removed the long carton that had holes to show its contents were intact. He read the writing, but it seemed like nonsense to him. "A dozen grade-A medium white eggs."

"Are they Captains?" Mork wondered, even more appalled at the thought of these prisoners being his superiors. He carefully removed them from the carton and placed them in a bowl. "Anybody there?" he asked in his normal Orkian voice. "Little Comrades, you must resist your oppressors!" He shook his head sadly. "As much as I like Mindy, it is against inter-galactic rules to eat spacemen." These Earthlings are crazy, he thought. Apparently they will eat anything. He could understand now why Orson had sent him to Earth. It certainly did give Mork a sense of how important illegal words are, to realize that not having them meant you could find yourself eating spacemen. And for breakfast, no less!

But he couldn't understand why, once he had released these grade-A brothers from the prison, they weren't hatching to tell him how it had happened, or, at least, flying home to what must be a very tiny planet. He picked one up and held it out at arm's length, not wishing to be overcome by *limakook,* the exhaust fumes of its tiny engines. *Limakook,* even in small quantities, can make an Orkan so dizzy that even sleeping on a couch is comfortable by comparison. "Fly!" he said. "Be free!" And he let go of the egg.

What a horrible sight! The egg fell to the counter and cracked, a peculiar mess of yellow liquid oozing out. Mork was in despair. He grabbed a sponge and wiped the egg into the sink. He turned on the water and looked solemn. "Burial at sea is some compensation," he said to the poor spaceman. "I'll notify your next of kin." Mork leaned over the bowl of eggs and said, "Your friend bit the big one. The cold machine must have placed you in a state of suspended animation. I was foolish not to consider that possibility."

Mork considered the problem. He could use his *bloink* to heat the eggs up, but he was afraid that unless he was precise he might cook them. The thought was disgusting. "I know what I'll do. I'll place you around the room," he said, taking out an egg and placing it on a seat cushion. "When you warm up, you'll revive and be free to fly." Mork took the remaining ten eggs and put them under the couch cushions, the chairs, in the plant soil— any spot that looked cozy. "You people are really short," he said. He was very upset with Mindy about all this. Of course, as an Orkan, his being very upset didn't mean he was angry or ready to quarrel with her. He was disappointed that she could understand so little about life. But he couldn't really blame her; she was a victim of a deprived upbringing. He would enlighten her and explain that to eat these spacemen was no different from eating him.

His thoughts were interrupted by a loud knocking on the door. Mindy had said nothing about this situation. And Mork, always ready to learn and have a new experience, opened the door. Deputy

Sheriff Tilwick was standing there, fulfilling his promise to Fred. Tilwick was still in uniform, glaring down at Mork.

"Hi, Smokey," Mork said, as he had heard an Earthling speak on television. He realized now that the television would be a handy guide to how he should behave. "I'm Mork," he said brightly. He put out his hand in the Orkian manner, his fingers spread. Although Mindy had told him not to do that, it was still too much of a habit to break.

Tilwick was soothed for a moment by Mork's friendly look. And he found himself starting to shake the offered hand, but when he saw how strangely Mork's fingers were placed, he drew himself up again. He remembered what a scoundrel this hippie in his overalls and yellow T-shirt was. "I'm not a member of your fraternity, kid. I don't want any of your secret handshakes."

Tilwick strode into the apartment, brushing past Mork roughly, and looked around the room. "Is Mindy McConnell here?"

Mork loved Tilwick. He was just like a real Smokey from television. Yes, this Earthling concept of having real life in a box was very interesting. "No," Mork said. "She's at a place called 'work.' A strange concept having something to do with green paper."

Tilwick stared at Mork. The way this hippie talked! He was even more obnoxious than the ones who used slang all the time.

"Strange, indeed," Mork went on, "but she seems to enjoy it."

Tilwick nodded. He had this wise guy's number. "Uh-huh. And I suppose you don't like to work."

Mork raised his shoulders, as he had seen a

television Earthling do, only he forgot to lower them. "Wouldn't know."

"You've probably never worked, right?"

Mork finally let his shoulders down. "Never tried it."

Boy, this guy has really got his nerve. He actually looks proud that he's never worked. "I see," Tilwick said. "You just sponge off of Mindy?"

"Oh, no," Mork said. "We've never taken a bath together."

He's so zonked out by drugs that he can't understand the simplest thing, Tilwick thought, despairing for the nation's young. "I *mean,*" he said angrily, "you live off her. I've met your type before, and I think you're about the lowest form of life."

There they go again, Mork thought. They have so little knowledge of science. Every little Orkling knew what the lowest form of life was. "You should take a course in biology," Mork said gently. "The lowest forms of life are the *Swig,* the *Nelf,* and the *Hibengie.*"

Tilwick would have liked to bust this wiseguy on the head. "Don't pull that intellectual stuff on me. I couldn't go to college because I was too busy keeping things safe for lazy punks like you."

Punk? Mork searched his memory cells for the word's meaning.

"I'm a personal friend of the McConnells," Tilwick said. "And I don't want to see Mindy hurt."

"Mindy hurt?" Mork was alarmed. "What's the matter with her?"

"There won't be anything the matter with her as soon as you clear out of here. So take off, all right?"

Mork was terribly confused. Something had happened to Mindy because of him. And now they wanted him to take off, which was impossible. His flying egg ship had returned to Ork. "I just landed," Mork said. He could use a good strong flower right now.

Tilwick was pleased. He had shaken this guy, all right. His eyes were darting nervously around. Tilwick stuck out his chest even more and glared. "Look, buddy, I can make it pretty rough on you. See this uniform?"

An idea glimmered in Mork's mind. He switched to his Orkian voice. "Are you from Space Patrol?"

Tilwick stepped away from Mork. Maybe this guy isn't on drugs, Tilwick thought. Maybe this guy's a fruit. "Are you putting me on?" he asked.

Mork was amazed again by the wit of these humans. "Ha! Ha!" he quacked. "No, it would be difficult to put you on. You're not even hollow."

Tilwick was really disturbed now. This poor fellow was really out of it. He nodded slowly and smiled at Mork, ready to go for his gun.

Mork continued to use his speeded-up Orkian voice. "Did Orson send you to help me save my friends, the eggs?"

Tilwick looked around to make sure that this guy Orson wasn't here. Meanwhile, he nodded slowly at Mork, hoping he would say more.

"They have been badly frozen," Mork said.

Tilwick was getting quite scared. He had never really met anyone as nutty as this. He was backing away from Mork when he bumped into a chair and fell into it, right on top of one of the eggs that Mork had put there. He heard the crack and felt the cool liquid spread on the back of his trousers. He jumped up.

Mork's heart would have skipped a beat or leaped into his mouth—if he had a heart to do such things. This was the second death he had witnessed in one morning. He rushed over to the chair and said to the squashed egg, "You *nimnul!* Didn't you see him coming?" Mork turned to the other eggs and pleaded, "How can I help you if you won't help yourselves?"

Tilwick knew that either this kid was on a very powerful drug or he was as crazy as a person could be. He pulled out his gun and said, "Okay, kid, now settle down."

"I can't sit down," Mork said. "They won't fly away. The cold machine is very powerful."

"Well, then, just take it easy and stand there quietly."

Mork looked down at his feet to see how they were making noise. They weren't. He couldn't understand these Earthlings. They froze space-men and asked him to do ridiculous things like stand without making a sound.

Tilwick, keeping his eyes on Mork, picked up the telephone and called the sheriff's office. "Billy? Tilwick here. Listen, I've a young man here—oh, I guess in his early twenties—who's a real grape-fruit. You know what I meant? Yeah, yeah. Oh, no, much worse than that. What should I do, take him to the hospital?"

On the other end of the line, Billy, the sheriff, said, "Well, who's the complainant? A relative?"

"Just me, Billy," Tilwick answered. "The guy thinks eggs can fly, and he gets upset if you sit on one."

Billy thought about that. "Why would anyone sit on one?"

"Never mind about that. It's too long a story to tell ya. But I'm with the guy right now, and he's obviously crazy."

"Well, to have him committed, you gotta have a relative or a spouse. Or if he's committed a crime or exposed himself. What has he done?"

Tilwick looked at Mork, standing still and not making a sound.

"Well, he's hidden a lot of eggs around an apartment."

Billy's voice got angry. "Tilwick, are you loaded? What kind of a crime is that? Upholstery murder?"

"Billy," Tilwick said, his voice becoming strained, "this guy is really crazy, or he's tripping on some incredible drug."

"Well, if he's got drugs you can bring him in."

Tilwick looked at Mork. He's probably got at least one stick of marijuana, he told himself. "Hold on for a second," he told Billy. He walked up to Mork and said gently, "I'm gonna frisk you. Don't get upset."

"I cannot become upset," Mork explained. "I don't have any emotions."

Jesus! Tilwick thought to himself. And Billy doesn't think this guy is crazy! Tilwick ran his hands up and down Mork, who began to make Orkian noises that were merely reflexes having to do with their complicated physical structure.

"Klut, Bezoop. Fraz! Klut?"

Tilwick stopped and glared at Mork. "Cut that out."

Mork looked around. "What is it you wish me to cut for you?"

Tilwick sighed. So did Mork. "I mean, stop making those noises."

Mork was astonished once more by the impossible demands of these Earthlings. "If you persist in this hand-touching ritual, I cannot stop myself."

"What are you trying to tell me?"

"I agree with you, Smokey. These cultural exchanges are very difficult."

This was hopeless, Tilwick thought. "Do you have any identification?" he asked.

Mork nodded. "Many. My face, my clothing, my joint here," he said, pointing to the knuckle on his *bloink*.

"All, right," Tilwick said, furious. "I've had enough. Turn around."

Mork immediately did as he was asked.

"Put your hands behind your back." While Mork complied, Tilwick brought out his handcuffs and fastened them to Mork's wrists. "Now, don't move," he said, returning to the phone. "Listen, Billy, he doesn't have drugs, but he also doesn't have *anything:* no identification, no money. I'm gonna bring him in on a vagrancy or a John Doe charge, and then you can judge for yourself what a nut he is."

"I hope you know what you're doing, Tilwick."

"I do," he said and hung up firmly. That Billy has no spirit, he thought. "Okay, fella, now you come along nice and quietly."

✳✳✳

11

Mork had been thinking carefully on his trip to the police station. Since television was real, then he knew what was happening. He was being taken to see that bald-headed man in New York, or the one with flat hair in Hawaii. If he was lucky, then maybe he would get to meet the policewoman who liked to drink wine so much. He would have to get Perry Mason to defend him, unless, of course, it was Ironside whom he was being taken to. What really worried him was that Mindy might be in serious trouble. Smokey had said something about her being hurt, and he was sure that if she was in trouble it was because of him.

That would have bothered a human, no doubt, but it was an especially troubling thought for an Orkan. They were horrified at the thought of hurting people, whether indirectly or even unintentionally. Orkian respect for other life is limitless. Mork could have broken free of the handcuffs and disarmed Tilwick. Why, he could even kill Tilwick in a flash. But because Mork is an Orkan, he might as well not be able to do those things. Not for many *bleams* had an Orkan killed even the smallest *Swig*, *Nelf*, or *Hibengie*—not intentionally, at least. Besides, Mork was unhappy. Yes, he was feeling an emotion—not quite the way a human would, but, nevertheless, he was moved. The death of the eggs had been horrible, and he blamed himself for it. And now he might be responsible for something hurting Mindy. Emotions are not good for Orkans, especially bad emotions, and their effect is to rob Orkans of their will. Mork didn't feel like even lifting his *bloink* an inch, much less do something so vigorous as break his handcuffs off and escape from Tilwick.

Mork went with Tilwick quietly, hardly even looking at the streets while Tilwick drove him to the jail. Tilwick took him to the holding cells where they kept drunks, vagrants, and people who have committed crimes just before they are sent to prison. The cells were large and had two bunks in each, so they could accommodate four people. The jail was also the sheriff's office, and there was a man who handled the radio communications from the patrols and a deputy who looked after the prisoners, and, of course, in his own office, the sheriff. Tilwick waved away the deputy, who said, "Hey, what are you doing here? I thought you were off duty." He took Mork on into the sheriff's office.

"Here he is, sir."

The sheriff looked up from his newspaper and glanced at Mork. "He looks harmless enough."

"Ask him who is and where he comes from," Tilwick suggested.

The sheriff looked at Mork expectantly. "Well, son?" The sheriff was in his early sixties, with a full head of white hair, and watery brown eyes that looked long and slowly at people.

Mork was more and more unwilling to do anything. He stood there quietly.

"Where do you come from?" the sheriff asked, putting down his bifocals.

"From Ork," he said.

"What was that?" the sheriff said, turning his head slightly, as if he needed to have his ear more in line with the speaker.

"Ork," Tilwick said sarcastically. "Have you ever heard of such a place?"

"Is that a town in this state?" the sheriff asked.

"*Nin, nin,*" Mork said. "It's well beyond the Milky Way."

Tilwick smiled at the sheriff, as if to say, I told you so.

The sheriff frowned and sat up in his chair. "What's your name, son?"

"Mork."

"Not where you come from. Your name."

"No, no," Tilwick explained eagerly. "He comes from Ork, but his name is Mork."

The sheriff looked at Tilwick as if maybe the deputy was crazy. "Thanks for clearing that up." He turned to Mork again. "Do you have a wallet, son? You know, some papers that might tell us something about you."

"*Nin, nin,*" Mork said. "We don't use paper. Our minds recall everything perfectly, and we communicate mentally such data as that. And I can't pay you in paper, but I have plenty of sand."

Tilwick nodded. "See what I mean, sir? Now,

I've searched him and he certainly doesn't have anything. So we can hold him on a John Doe, right? Take his prints and—"

"Tilwick," the sheriff said curtly, "I know the procedure. I've only been doing this for thirty-five years. You go ahead with that and we'll get Dr. Litney in here to examine him. If he okays it, then we'll have a sanity hearing, and they'll decide if he goes to a fruit farm."

Mork thought about that for a long time. He hardly paid any attention to the fuss that was made over his not having a fingerprint on his *bloink*. They kept talking about something called plastic surgery. But this fruit-farm business was most strange. Is that punishment on Earth? Mork wondered. Mork couldn't decide whether prisoners washed the fruit or ate it. Eating it would really be frightening.

The cell was rather a nice place, Mork thought. Not horribly bright and dustless like other Earth places. It wasn't nearly as pleasant as Mindy's attic, of course. That was too much to hope for. He asked Tilwick where Mindy was just before they put him in the cell, but Tilwick said something even more puzzling. "She's at the store, selling music. Don't worry about her. You just relax. And stop calling me Smokey."

So Mork was left alone in his cell to think. But he couldn't relax. He walked around his cell wondering what a store and what selling music was. Had she become someone who sells something illegal? he thought with horror. Music on Ork was always of dubious legality. Only *Grenzel*, the tune that Earthphones play, and *Froppy*, are legal songs. The others had been outlawed because they provoked emotion. Though most emotion that music creates is considered harmless by Orkans, some songs had caused awful things to occur, such as a craze that flourished during the *Tet-Krell*, roughly the Orkian Middle Ages. In those horrible days, when Orkans waged war and ate living things, Orkans often gathered in bright places that were very clean and danced to music.

Until this morning, Mork would never have believed Mindy was capable of such a thing. But it is true that, when he discovered that morning that she was capable of freezing spacemen, or eggs, his faith in her had been shaken.

The whole morning experience had been exhausting. It was then that Mork noticed the bunks. He was struck by admiration for Earthlings. "A king-sized *Joz!*" he said with delight and promptly swung up to the upper bunk and hung from it by his feet, his head resting gently on the lower bunk, his body bent in a way that would have hurt a human badly.

Mork
&
Mindy

Mork

Mindy

"In the beginning . . ."

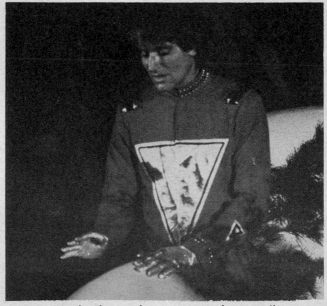

"Maybe this one has my missing luggage."

"You must learn to dress like an earthling."

"You teach me to behave like an earth person and I'll teach you about ORK."

"Na-no, na-no."

Mindy to the rescue

"No, Mork, I'm not rejecting you."

"Na-no, na-no."

Mork learns to cook

A piece of earth food

Killer Baloney

Mork loves earth television

Earthling fingers are different than Orkians

Mork and Eugene

Mork and friend

"Shazbot."

"Do not worry—I will save you."

Strange clothes for earthlings

Fred, Mindy's father

Cora, Mindy's
grandmother

* * *

12

Mindy had spent most of the morning trying to get her father alone. But Fred had several lessons to teach. There were two rooms at the back of the store where Fred gave piano and violin lessons, and he waited in there between students, not responding to Mindy's knocks. After his second lesson, he came out. He looked terrible. His eyes were bloodshot and he walked as if the room were a boat in a stormy sea. He kept steadying himself on objects as he passed them. When Mindy tried to speak with him, he shut his eyes and winced.

"Daddy, do you have a hangover?" Mindy asked, surprised. Her father had never gotten drunk as far as she could remember.

Fred opened his eyes slightly. They looked hurt, not only because of the red lines, but because they were sad and wounded. "What do *you* think?"

"I think you have a hangover."

Fred closed his eyes again. "I'm not talking to you."

"Daddy, please, listen to me. I want you to come home with me at lunchtime."

Fred rubbed his forehead. "Why? Have you thrown him out?"

"Uh." Mindy looked guilty under Fred's questioning stare.

"Well?" he said, impatient.

"I want you to be there so that we—"

"Forget it!" Fred immediately regretted having yelled at her. It made his head hurt. His tongue felt like it was three sizes too large for his mouth. "Leave me alone," he said. "Isn't it enough that you've broken my heart?"

Cora had been selling on the other side of the store. "Now, this is the perfect axe for your band. No distortion and lots of volume. In fact, you can't turn it all the way up or you'll bust every zit in the place." But her customers, two long-haired teenagers, had only listened for as long as they did because they were amazed that this woman in her sixties knew so much about rock music. She now joined Fred and Mindy by saying, "Why don't you stop avoiding her? Mindy's a young girl and she has to experience life."

"Do you approve of her living with a man?" Fred demanded.

"Approve? No," Cora said, and Fred began to smile. "Envy? Yes." And Fred closed his eyes both from frustration and illness. "Come off it, Fred," Cora said cheerfully. "She's not any different, is she? This is a new world for women. It's not like the old days when if they behaved for a minute for their pleasure everybody stoned them to death."

"What difference does it make how the world feels?" Fred pleaded. "It's how *I* feel that matters."

"Cora," Mindy said, "thanks, but no thanks. Dad,

if you would only come home with me, I could explain the whole thing so that you would still be happy and feel your little girl still lives."

"How can you do that?" Fred said, suspicious. "You're only trying to trick me into meeting that— that punk. You're crazy enough to think that I'll like him and forget my objections."

Mindy was shaking her head and trying to interrupt. "Dad, that's not it—"

"Oh, yes, it is!" Fred yelled. "I won't be fooled! Even if he were President of the United States, I wouldn't approve of your living with him!"

"He's crazy," Cora decided and walked away.

Mindy was about to argue again when the door opened and Fred called out happily, "Tilwick! My good friend! How are you?"

Tilwick glanced at Mindy nervously. He knew that Mindy couldn't be in love with that lunatic, and he had decided she was merely being kind by giving him somewhere to stay. After all, he had a daughter. He knew how much girls liked to take in every stray. He had lived with a house full of animals his daughter rescued from the cold, cruel outdoors. Tilwick knew that Mindy would be furious with him for trying to get Mork committed to a mental clinic. So Tilwick walked past her and whispered in Fred's ear, "I have to talk to you."

Mindy was made suspicious by Tilwick's glances in her direction as he walked off with Fred, so she edged her way after them, listening hard.

"Did you scare him off?" Fred asked.

"You, uh, well, you won't have to worry about him." Looking at Mindy made Tilwick feel guilty about what he had done, just like when he forced his daughter to give up the wounded bird she found one weekend.

"So you scared him off?"

"Uh." Now Tilwick was so ashamed he couldn't even bear to tell Fred.

"He was yellow, was he? A couple of words from authority and he runs." Fred shook his head with disgust. "What a heel!"

"That's not the way it happened," Tilwick confessed.

Fred stared at him and became worried. "Well, what in heaven did you do?"

By now Mindy was very close to them, and Tilwick whispered the news that he had put Mork in jail as a preparation to having him committed.

"What!?" Fred was appalled. For all his tough talk about having Mork's head cut off, he wished the young man no harm. "I just wanted you to get rid of him—not do *that!*"

"I didn't want to," Tilwick said, almost whining. "I had to do my duty. No matter how harmless those nuts may seem, they turn violent in a minute. You wouldn't want that, would you?"

"Is this about Mork?" Mindy asked, fear rising inside her.

Both men stood and looked stupidly at her.

"What have you done!" she yelled, almost hysterical.

"Mindy," Tilwick said, no longer convinced that he was right, "I just went to your apartment to scare him away. I know, I know, that's not my job, but keeping lunatics off the street *is*. When I saw him there, talking to the eggs and claiming he was from Outer Space, I just had to do my duty!"

Mindy was almost too scared to ask. "What,"

she said, her voice full of threat, "was your duty, Deputy Tilwick?"

"I know he's your friend. I know you weren't doing what your dad thought. It's a nice idea, Mindy, but professionals—"

"Answer my question!" Mindy said, her eyes burning at Tilwick.

"I had to take him in," Tilwick admitted. Mindy groaned and Tilwick swallowed before he went on. "He's bonkers," Tilwick pleaded, looking at Fred. "The shrink is coming to examine him, and if he thinks it's necessary, there'll be a sanity hearing soon."

Mindy began to cry. Fred went over to her, but she pushed him away, groaning as she said, "Are you happy now? Is that what you wanted?"

"How did I know he was going to do that?" Fred protested. "I was drunk. He came here last night when I was drunk and I told him about you and Mork—"

"Will you listen to me!" Mindy yelled, still crying. "I've tried to tell you over and over. There's nothing between us. I was just giving him a place to stay, because he's—"

Tilwick broke in: "You know how it is, Fred. This guy is like a kid. He's got no money and he thinks he's from another planet. She felt sorry for him."

"But he's not crazy!" Mindy shouted.

Tilwick felt sorry for Mindy. She was just like his daughter, unable to believe that some cases really are hopeless. Fred looked at Tilwick questioningly. "How about it? I met the kid. He seemed like a wiseguy, but not crazy."

"Fred," Tilwick pleaded, "he thinks he's from another planet."

"But—" Mindy began. The two men looked at her. She waved her hands in frustration and said, "We have to get him out, Dad. We have to bail him out."

Fred thought of his meager bank account. He looked doubtful.

"You have to, Dad!" Mindy said, her face reddening. "You got Mork into this mess, so it's your responsibility to get him out."

"How about it, Tilwick?" Fred said. He had made up his mind that only through helping Mindy could he regain her respect and love.

"Well," Tilwick said, "for today, there's nothing you can do. He's got to be examined by the psychiatrist."

"I've got to see him," Mindy said, "before the psychiatrist does!"

"Now, surely you can arrange that," Fred said threateningly to his friend Tilwick. But his friend backed away, looking uncertain. "Tilwick, if you arrested him, I'm pretty sure you can get a visitor in to see him."

This sure had been a confusing day for Tilwick. He still hadn't gotten to bed, for one thing. But he obliged. Mindy had succeeded in making him feel like a villain, and during the drive to the jail, he found himself planning ways to convince the sanity hearing that Mork wasn't crazy. Mindy had told Tilwick that Mork liked to kid people and that his placement of eggs all around her apartment was an old fraternity prank. Tilwick tried to believe her and Fred did, thinking to himself that that was just the sort of thing an unemployed hippie would do.

But when Tilwick asked Mindy where Mork came from, if not from another planet, Mindy was stumped. "Uh, from New York City," she said in desperation.

And it must have been a good choice, because Fred nodded and said, "Of course."

Even Tilwick looked impressed. "Yeah, that makes sense."

At the jail, the same deputy who was on duty earlier looked at Tilwick with amazement. "What are you trying for, cop of the century?"

"Look, this is Mindy McConnell, a good friend of the John Doe in there. I'm gonna take her in for a quick chat with him."

"What for? Has the chief cleared this?"

"Um." Tilwick's eyes wandered as he tried to think of something. "She can help with the identification."

The deputy smiled slyly. "I see," he said, leering. "But I thought he was in on a psycho."

Tilwick took Mindy's arm and began walking past, saying, "A little of this, a little of that. You know how my arrests are." The deputy laughed and forgot about asking any more questions. Tilwick mumbled something to the jailer and went on into the cell area. Mindy said, "Let me go in alone, okay?"

Tilwick looked doubtful.

"Please," Mindy said, trying to look as pretty and young as she could, and she could look very pretty and young.

"All right," Tilwick said, his heart melted by her eyes. "But don't do anything foolish."

Mindy promised she wouldn't. When she reached Mork's cell, she was very glad she had convinced Tilwick to let her go in alone, because Mork was sound asleep, hanging upside down from the bunk. "Mork!" she whispered intently. "Mork!" she said again.

Orkans wake up quickly and always by jumping immediately to their feet. Mindy backed away, she was so startled by Mork's backflip. "Mindy," Mork said in a tone that sounded unexcited to Mindy, but that was close to a shout of joy for an Orkan. "You are well?" he asked.

"Mork, how are *you*?"

"I am distressed, my Earth friend."

"I know," Mindy said, looking sympathetic. "I'm sorry about this. My father went crazy and got his friend Tilwick to—"

Mork was shaking his head with super sadness. When Mindy stopped speaking at this unexpected sight, he said, "I am sorry to hear of your father's mental illness, but I am referring to your treatment of spacemen."

Mindy stared. "My what?"

"I know that as a primitive people you eat many living things, but I had no suspicion that you went so far as to consume intelligent life."

"Mork," Mindy said, almost ready to cry from frustration, "we don't have a lot of time, so could you tell me what you're talking about?"

"I am speaking of your placing spacemen in the cold machine—in that box with the title, 'Grade-A medium white eggs.' "

Mindy instantly realized the situation. "Mork, those aren't spacemen. They just happen to be shaped like spacemen from your planet. On Earth, they are eggs. I mean, they are the unborn—uh, let me see, how can I explain this? They are produced by a chicken, an animal. They are not intelligent life; in fact, by the time I buy them, they are not alive at all."

Mork put his finger in the air. "Ah! Is that why they couldn't fly? I thought the cold machine had placed them in a state of suspended animation."

"No, no." Mindy breathed deeply. "Anyway, I promise I'll never eat them again if it bothers you."

Mork tilted his head to one side. He was impressed by this. He hadn't realized that humans were capable of reforming their behavior. He had assumed that they were victims of uncontrollable passions. He felt much better, though, learning that he hadn't been the cause of two deaths this morning. "But," he said, "I have also heard that you sell music."

Mindy frowned. She didn't know what that was about, but she didn't have the time to explain all these things now. "We'll talk about that later, Mork. You have to listen carefully now. A doctor will be coming to see you, and you must be careful not to say anything about your coming from Outer Space. Pretend that you come from New York City."

"Is New York like Ork?"

"No. You must pretend that you are a human. Don't use your finger to do anything that a human can't do."

"Why do I have to see this doctor? I would prefer to leave with you."

"No, Mork. If you do that, then everybody will be looking for you and eventually we'd have to tell them you're from Outer Space."

"What would be wrong with that?"

"Mork, you don't realize what they'd do to you."

Mork nodded. "*Yug*," he said, the daytime Orkian "yes." "They'll force me to become a celebrity.

Movies, fame, stuck in a box on 'Hollywood Squares. It's disgusting. I saw *A Star Is Born.*"

"Mork," Mindy said, "that's the good side of it."

Mork was astonished. "It is?"

"Oh, yes. You'd never have any privacy. Everybody'll be saying *Na-No, Na-No.* They'll be dolls, games. It'll be like living in a zoo."

Mork's eyes widened with fear. Orkans are afraid of crowds. The record attendance for the *Kerkle Bowl,* the most important athletic event of the year on Ork, is twenty-one Orkans. It was called an unruly mob by their one sportswriter. "*Shazbot!*" he said, the only legal Orkian swear word—legal because it has no meaning.

"And the government," Mindy said, "you have no idea what they might do. They'll probably think you're a threat to our security. They'll lock you up and try to find out how your technology works. The Russians will probably demand that you be given over to the United Nations for study. They might do anything—they could put you in a bottle."

"Oh, no," Mork said. "My grandfather was a bottle. He died a broken man."

"I'd probably never see you again," Mindy said, too worried to react to Mork's strange remark.

"They'd make me invisible?" Mork asked, frightened again. Ork scientists had played around with invisibility at one time. At first, their experiments had gone well, but as they made more and more Orkans invisible, they had trouble finding them, and they lost many. The program came under heavy criticism and was canceled in disgrace. Apparently, after a few days of invisibility, Orkans would forget who they were and fade away for good.

"No, they'd take you away."

"I would not like that, Mindy-Earthling," Mork said unemotionally, but it moved Mindy. She felt so badly that she had caused him all this trouble.

"Okay, now, listen. This doctor will be examining you because he thinks you might be insane. Do you know what I mean by that?"

Mork put his index finger up in the air. "It means I am *Ka-bloink*."

"That's right. So I want you to act like a human would."

Tilwick's voice broke in. "Mindy," he said from the door leading to the cells, "your time's up."

"Okay," she said and turned back to Mork. "Remember—just like a human." She smiled at Mork and said, "I'll get you out of here later—by tonight."

Mork nodded. "Okay," he said. "Good-bye."

Mindy left feeling reassured. After all, Mork had said good-bye just like any human would. Once she was back with Tilwick, she began pestering him about how they could get Mork out of police custody. Tilwick said that it was impossible until they got some proof of Mork's identity. "Oh," Mindy said, crushed. Tilwick took her and Fred to Mindy's apartment. She was silent all the way and the two men were afraid to talk, they both felt so guilty.

Just before Tilwick left them off, Mindy asked him if she could see Mork again that night. When Tilwick began to say it was impossible, Fred glared at him, and he changed his mind. "Okay," he said with a sigh, "at nine o'clock, when my shift begins."

Mindy was relieved again. During the ride home she had figured out a way to get Mork identification. She wasn't sure if it would work, but seeing Mork was the first step—provided, of course, that Mork didn't do anything outrageous with the psychiatrist. Like tell him his grandfather was a bottle. Or *Kerkle* his chest.

*** *** ***

13

After Mindy left, Mork thought carefully about what she had said. She had certainly worried him. He had no idea that humans would react that way to discovering he was from another planet. For Orkans, people from other planets is as common an event as people from other states are in America. So Mork was bent upon fooling this earth doctor, which shouldn't be hard, he told himself. After all, Mork was an advanced form of life, and this doctor was ignorant of even the most ordinary medical techniques, such as deep-cloning. Deep-cloning is the Orkian method of psychoanalysis. A clone of a troubled Orkan is made and placed in a room. The clone has a perfect memory of every event that has occurred to the original Orkan. When the clone describes the traumatic event that has made the original ill, doctors go to the original and make the event illegal. It had once happened to Mork. He had been upset because he learned that his father, an eye-dropper, had run off with another microscope glass. A tart with infrared glass, Mork was told. His clone pinpointed that event as the cause for Mork's problem, which was that he kept walking into mirrors. The cure was simple. Doctors made it illegal for Mork to say the Orkian word for glass.

So Mork tried to remember everything he had heard on television about earth life. He was busy doing that when Dr. Litney, the psychiatrist, arrived. Dr. Litney was in his late thirties, a big man who carried a briefcase filled with I.Q. tests. Otherwise, he looked very ordinary. He smiled at Mork in an insincere way and said, "Hello. My name is Dr. Litney." He took out a pad and waited for Mork to say something. When a minute passed, Litney realized he would have to proceed with care. "So, what is your name?" he asked, overly polite.

"Mork."

"Is that M-O-R-C-K?"

Mork had no idea what that meant. He hadn't watched "Seasame Street" and so he knew little of our alphabet. He took a guess and nodded yes.

Dr. Litney wrote that down. "Now, I understand that you don't have a last name?"

Mork knew about last names. He had seen a documentary about feminism and listened carefully to all that talk about maiden names. "My married name is Ricardo," he said, using his favorite television character's last name. Mork had spent a lot of time watching the reruns of "I Love Lucy" when he was on Ork.

The doctor looked up. He peered at Mork's serious face. He suspected him of kidding. "Now," he said, leaning close and smiling, "I know that fraternities sometimes go in for pretty crazy stunts. I was young once, too, you know."

"You don't look a day over thirty," Mork said, remembering that Fonzie had told him flattery was important.

"Thank you," Litney said, pleased. But then he caught himself and wondered if Mork was being a wiseguy. "All right, look, what's all this about your being from another planet?"

"Just a joke. Ha! Ha!" Mork barked, throwing his head back and slapping his knee so hard that it made a resounding noise.

Litney wrote down something and said, "Well, now that the joke is over, could you tell me where you were born?"

"In Cuba," Mork said.

"So your name is Mork Ricardo and you come from Cuba? Are you a citizen of the United States?"

"Oh, *si*. I mean, yes I am."

"And when were you born?"

Mork had to think about that one. "In the 1950s," he said at last.

"Well, *when* in the 1950s? What year? What month? What day?"

Mork put his hands on his head and rocked it from side to side. "I have to ask my wife, Lucy. I don't know."

"You can't remember when you were born?"

"Well, I know roughly," Mork said. "I was a summer replacement. Sometime in the early '50s. Our records are not in the best condition," Mork said, thinking of all that intergalactic interference.

"Oh, yes," Litney said, it suddenly dawning on him. "The Revolution. I forgot." Litney made a note. "So, I gather that you are married?"

"Oh, yes, and I have a baby."

"And your wife's name is—"

"Lucille," Mork said, watching the doctor as he wrote it down. "And my son's name is little Morky."

Litney finished writing all that down. "All right, I'm glad the kidding is over. Now, I'm just going to do a few simple tests and then maybe we can check on all this. I gather you don't have any identification?"

"What do you mean?" Mork said. He remembered his earlier answers to Tilwick hadn't been taken well. Mork was being cautious because he knew that this *was* going very well.

"Well, a birth certificate, a passport, a draft card. You know—checks, et cetera."

"Ah!" Mork thought quickly. "I left them with my friends."

"Who are they?" Dr. Litney said with interest, his pen poised to write down the information.

"Fred and Ethel Mertz."

The doctor looked up. Something about this was not right. He couldn't put his finger on it. He looked at Mork to see if the young man was smirking or showing some sign that he might be still joking. But Mork's face was serious, his eyes clear and unblinking. "Well, can you get in touch with them and have them bring your identification here?"

"Not right now," Mork said. "I have to see my other friend first."

"Who is that?"

"Mindy," Mork said.

"Oh, yes," Litney said, staring at the sheet the deputy had given him. "Mindy McConnell. That's whose apartment you were arrested at. Okay, very good. Now, let's get to these tests." Dr. Litney opened his briefcase and took out Rorschach cards. Rorschach cards are blotches of ink that suggest images. From the kinds of images people make out of them, psychiatrists can evaluate the person. Litney showed the first one, which looked like two naked women to him.

Mork was delighted. "Postcards!" he said, amazed. "That's a lovely drawing."

"What are you talking about?" Litney said.

"That drawing of a *Grewtz*—" Mork caught himself. Humans don't have *Grewtz*'s. "Ha! Ha!" he barked. "A little humor to brighten up the day. I am very sorry."

Uses bad jokes as a defense, Litney wrote down. "Okay, now let's get serious. What does this look like?"

"Ink on paper."

"No, no. Haven't you ever taken one of these tests before?"

Mork shook his head. "No. They don't have this in Cuba."

"Well, just try and imagine. Try and tell me what this might look like to you."

Mork stared at the drawing. Other than a *Grewtz*, it looked like someone spilled ink. "Okay," he said. "I've got it: spilled ink."

Litney controlled himself. This fellow had the most irritating manner, he thought. He teases with such a serious face. *Uncooperative on the Rorschach*, he wrote. "All right, let's try something else," he said, pulling out a board with holes set into it. The holes were of various shapes: squares, triangles, and the like. Litney placed the board on Mork's bunk and then handed him blocks of wood of various shapes. Each block of wood corresponded to one of the shapes on the board. Litney explained that to Mork, brought out a timer, and said, "When I say go, I want you to fit them in as quickly as you can." Litney set his timer and said, "Go!"

Mork considered the situation. He knew that Earth science was on a very different level from Ork's. But he had no television reference point for this. He had no idea of what an Earthling's notion of correct was. Perhaps they were *clonish* and thought that square fits into square, and so on. Perhaps they were a bit more advanced and had gotten as far as triangle into a rectangle. He was sure they didn't know that an octagon was as good as a circle. Well, he would take a guess. Mork picked up the square shape and watched Litney's eyes as he hovered over the square shape and then over the circle shape. There was more eye movement for the circle shape, so Mork decided that must be the right one. Mork took the square and easily fit it into the circle.

Litney exclaimed at the sight. It was impossible to do what Mork had just done. He grabbed the board away and tried to pull the block out. He pulled so hard that when he momentarily lost his grip, he fell off his chair.

"Are you hurt?" Mork asked.

"How did you do that?" Litney demanded. "It's impossible to do that!"

Mork was alarmed. "I thought you wanted it there," Mork said.

Litney got off the floor and pulled at the block again. It wouldn't budge. Mork could get it out, but he realized that if he did that, then the doctor would know something really strange was going on.

"You've ruined it," Litney said bitterly.

"I am most sorry." Mork hung his head very low.

"Now, you listen to me, Mr. Ricardo, I don't think this kidding around is very healthy behavior. I think you are behaving anti-socially. And unless you stop right now, I'm going to recommend that there be a sanity hearing."

"I am very sorry, Doctor. I will try to improve."

Litney stared at Mork. His eyes certainly gave the impression of honesty. He'd give the boy one more chance. "All right." Litney reseated himself and glanced at Mork as he looked down at a sheet of paper with words on one side and blanks on the other. "Now, I'm going to say words at random and you should say the first word that comes into your head. It doesn't matter whether it makes any sense. Just say what comes into your mind. Like, if I say 'black,' you might say 'white.' All right? Do you understand?"

"Yes," Mork said solemnly.

"Dog," Litney said.

"Alpo."

Litney looked up. "What?"

Mork spoke louder. "Alpo."

Litney sighed. He wrote the answer down. "Woman."

"Chanel Number Five."

Litney dropped his pen. "Are you going to give me the name of products for everything I say?"

"I was merely saying what came into my mind. You do not wish me to mention material things?"

"Those two items were the first things that came into your mind?"

Mork nodded.

Litney picked up his pen. "Well, try and come up with answers that are a little more human, all right?" Mork nodded at him and Litney cleared his throat, getting ready to say the next word.

Mork, however, interpreted this noise as Litney's next question, and he promptly answered, "Sore throat."

Dr. Litney could take no more.

"That's it," he said, standing up. He picked up his briefcase and began to jam his tests in. "I've had enough. You're in a lot of trouble, Mr. Ricardo. I'm going to recommend that we have the sanity hearing. This kind of persistent anti-social behavior indicates to me that it might be dangerous to have you out there. I'm not sure at what point you cross that line between being aggressively verbal and just being plain physically aggressive." And with that incomprehensible speech, from Mork's point of view, Dr. Litney left. The poor man was so distracted and angry that he forgot to tell the sheriff that he had found out who and where Mork came from. He merely said, "I'm recommending we have the hearing. You'd better find him a lawyer."

The poor kid, the sheriff thought. He picked up the phone and spoke with the District Attorney's office.

***

14

A few hours later, while Mork was being served his dinner, which he ate like a normal human, the D.A.'s office phoned back to say that the hearing would be held in two days and that a lawyer from the public defender's office had been assigned to Mork.

Shortly after that, Tilwick came in with Mindy. "Uh, Chief," he said, "this is Mindy McConnell."

The sheriff and Mindy exchanged greetings.

"I arrested that young man at her apartment. Now, he is apparently well known to her, and she claims that he is merely kidding."

The sheriff looked Mindy over carefully. She seemed too respectable to be up to anything. "Well, he kidded the psychiatrist so well that he told me to arrange the sanity hearing."

Tilwick had been afraid of that. Well, he'd have to keep Mindy calm and get her home quietly.

"When is the hearing?" Mindy asked.

"Friday morning," the sheriff answered.

"Let me talk with him. If I can talk with him, I assure you he'll prove to you who he is."

The sheriff eyed Mindy closely. He spoke softly to her. "Maybe you'd better tell me what this is all about, young woman. You'll feel better talking it out."

"It's nothing," Mindy insisted, and she pulled her arm away from Tilwick, who was urging her out. "It's just that Mork gets silly around authority and he starts kidding around, and he doesn't know when to stop." The two men didn't say anything. "Just give me ten minutes with him. Please," she said, her eyes pleading.

"I can't see any harm in that," the sheriff said, "especially if you can clear up his identity."

"Thank you," Mindy said, turning to go.

"And," the sheriff called after her, "you'd better tell him that if he's kidding, that he just might joke himself into a straitjacket."

"I will," Mindy promised. She went out, Tilwick escorting her to the cell. He left her there alone, as she asked. Mork was so glad to see her—Orkans easily become lonely—that his *bloink* almost hummed.

"Mork, what happened with the doctor?"

"*Shazbot!*" Mork said. "I have been considering that for many hours. I made up a good story, I thought."

"You told him you were from New York?"

"I told him I was born in Cuba and had moved to New York. I was clever. I remembered that program about the stranger who marries the redhead. So I used their name."

"Oh," Mindy groaned and leaned her head against the bars. "You told him you were Ricky Ricardo?"

"*Nox, nox,*" Mork said, using the most emphatic of the legal Orkian no's. Some of the illegal no's are so emphatic that just saying them creates quite a breeze. "I was not that *clonish*. I told him I was Mork Ricardo."

"Mork, don't you understand why that would make him think you were crazy?"

"But, Mindy-Earthling, that is not what made him *Ka-bloink*. He was nice to me about that. He told me that if I did well on the tests and could provide identification, saying I am Mork Ricardo, all would be well."

"Really?" Mindy said. "He believed that you were Mork Ricardo?"

"Yes," Mork said. "It was when I put the square block into the circular hole that he became upset."

Mindy rubbed her forehead in despair. Why hadn't the sheriff mentioned that Mork had said who he was?

"Mindy!" It was Tilwick, calling from the doorway. Mindy went over to him. "The shrink just called. He said he forgot to say that Mork had told him who he is."

Mindy nodded warily. Weren't they going to notice?

"Did you know he was married?" Tilwick asked. "He even has a kid."

Mindy went on nodding uncertainly. "He gave his name?" she asked.

"Sure," Tilwick said. "Ricardo. And he has a wife named Lucille. He's a Cuban. But he's got American citizenship. You knew all that?"

Mindy smiled and nodded. "Yep," she said quietly, trying not to laugh.

"He says he has friends, a Mr. and Mrs. Mertz, who can bring his identification here."

Mindy bit her lip before speaking. "Yeah, we were discussing that now. I think he can get hold of his passport. I was trying to find out what he did that got the psychiatrist upset."

"Okay," Tilwick said. "I guess I should have believed you. You know Latins—they like to kid around. Funny thing is, he doesn't look Spanish."

Ignoring that comment, Mindy said, "Let me go back and find out how to get in touch with his friends."

"Okay," Tilwick said. Mindy walked back to Mork's cell. She opened her purse and took out her passport. It had never been used; indeed, Mindy had never been out of the United States. But having a passport made her feel as if she had traveled all over. "Mork," she said, "this is a piece of identification. Can you change my name and this writing, and also the photograph?"

Mork looked at the small blue booklet. "Certainly. What would you wish me to change it to?"

"Well," Mindy said, pointing to the top line, "put down Mork Ricardo here." Mork pointed his *bloink* and there was a brief hum and Mindy's name disappeared. He pointed again and there was a funny noise.

"Excuse me," Mork said. He tapped his finger twice. "Ink gets sluggish," he explained and pointed again. There was a glow of light. Mork showed her the booklet.

Mork Ricardo was neatly printed. Mindy had him write in his sex, and they made up a date of birth, wrote in his wife's name, and also little Morky's. When they came to the photograph, Mork had some trouble. Photographs on Ork are quite different from what they are on Earth. They are almost completely black, a difference having to do with the Orkian eye, which becomes more clear-sighted the darker it gets. So the first two photographs Mork created of himself looked like pictures of dark closets with a dim figure in the middle. Mindy had quite a bit of trouble convincing Mork that on Earth those pictures were unviewable. And when he did his third version, though there was enough light, Mork had made the picture represent himself standing in a jail cell, the bars lining his face. But the fourth version was perfect. Mindy had him add his signature on the photograph, as well as the bottom of the page, and she also had him change the numbers of the passport, a precaution that really wouldn't help if the sheriff bothered to check them, since there would be no record of a Mork Ricardo in Washington. Mindy told Mork to stick to the story he had told the psychiatrist and to keep trying to behave like an Earthling.

"You are not taking me with you now?" Mork asked.

"First I have to show them the passport," she said. She assured him that he wouldn't have to stay any longer than one more night. But the fact was, Mindy had no idea if she could get Mork released. The legality of this situation had her confused. She went into the sheriff's office boldly, however. She didn't care how much trouble she got into trying to free Mork. It was completely her fault that he had gotten into this mess. If her father hadn't been so old-fashioned, Tilwick would never have seen Mork, much less put him away.

"Well, how'd it go?" the sheriff asked. Tilwick was with him. He also looked curiously at Mindy. What if they had noticed about the names? Mindy worried. As soon as she showed that passport, she would be committing fraud—at least. Well, now was not the time to think about that, she decided, and the less time she wasted trying to get Mork out, the less time they had to notice that he was more than some nutty hippie.

Mindy looked serious and apologetic. "I convinced him the joke wasn't very funny. And it turned out he had his passport with him all the time." Mindy tossed the blue booklet onto the sheriff's desk. "He had it hidden, uh, in his pants," she guessed, hoping that they hadn't searched Mork, which they hadn't, since this was merely a holding cell.

Tilwick and the sheriff were both surprised. When the sheriff opened up Mork's fake passport, Tilwick leaned over so much that the sheriff looked up at him and said, "Do you mind?"

"Sorry, Chief," Tilwick said.

The sheriff looked at it carefully and then checked its contents against the information Dr. Litney had called in. "Yeah, that checks out."

"Now, can I put him up at my apartment until the hearing?" Mindy said. "You can tell he's harmless, even if you won't believe me that he isn't crazy."

The sheriff had learned, during his thirty-five-year tenure as a police officer, that when you're unsure, the best thing to do is look smart and keep your mouth shut. So he stared and looked hard at Mindy. But as tough as he made himself look, he really didn't believe that this pretty, sweet young woman was up to anything bad. Besides, Tilwick had told the sheriff that he had known Mindy all of her life, and that she was a dutiful and intelligent daughter who had never done anything more illegal than cross the street on a red light.

Tilwick wasn't sure, however, that Mindy's suggestion was a good one. "You sure your father wouldn't get upset about that?" he asked. "I mean, having a married man stay at your apartment?"

Mindy almost forgot and asked Tilwick whom he was talking about. "Dad can sleep over, too, if he's so suspicious," she said, her eyes showing Tilwick that she wasn't thrilled about his part in all this. "We're going to need to have Mork out in order to find a doctor who will testify that he's sane and get in touch with his wife and son," Mindy said to the sheriff. "Can't you release him in my custody?"

The sheriff normally wouldn't agree to such a thing, but the look in Mindy's eyes told him he wouldn't have a minute's peace if he didn't give in. "Well, if Deputy Tilwick is willing to promise he'll check in with you twice a day and make sure Mork hasn't gone anywhere, then I guess I'll agree to it."

"Oh! Thank you!" Mindy said, rushing around the sheriff's desk and kissing him on the forehead. Tilwick looked away and the sheriff also lowered his head.

"That's all right. That's all right," he mumbled. "Uh, help her get Mork released and drive them to her apartment," the sheriff said to Tilwick.

Mindy put her finger to her lips when Tilwick brought Mork out. While they stood at the desk, waiting for the deputy to do the necessary paperwork, the sheriff came out and said to Mork, "Well, Mr. Ricardo, I hope you realize that this sort of joking around isn't a very smart thing to do."

Mindy nodded encouragingly to Mork. "Oh," she

said, "I'm sure he does. You're sorry about all this, aren't you, Mork?"

Mork put his hands to his head and rocked it back and forth. "*Ayie, Ayie! Sí*, I am so upset about it, I cannot tell you," he said with a Spanish accent.

The deputy looked up from the form he was filling out. "I have it down here that he doesn't have an occupation. Is that still how you want it to read?" he asked Mork.

"Well," Mork said, looking sneakily around the room, "I don't want you to let this get around, because if the papers get hold of this, I may not get that part I'm up for in that big new motion picture. But I am the headliner at the—"

Mindy interrupted: "At The Bitter End in Greenwich Village," she said.

"Oh," the sheriff said with a trace of disgust. "A rock star, huh?"

"Are we all finished?" Mindy said very loudly to drown out Mork, who was getting ready to sing "Babaloo."

"I guess," said the deputy behind the desk.

Mindy grabbed Mork's arm and dragged him out while he said, "If Lucy calls, tell her she can't have a part in the new picture. It wouldn't be good for little Morky to have both parents in show business," Mork went on to Tilwick as they got outside.

"Okay, Mork," Mindy said. "You've had a rough day. Why don't you just sit still and not bother talking?" This, of course, shut Mork up from telling about the last time he and Lucy and Fred and Ethel were in court. It was over a broken television. Mork realized now how tragic that particular program had been. For humans, a broken television is like being in exile, Mork thought. You are cut off completely from reality.

He was quiet during the ride home. Mindy had certainly done a wonderful thing, he thought, getting him out of the jail. Her sacrifice interested him. It was completely different behavior from an Orkan's. To defy authority on Ork was never done knowingly—and certainly not out of friendship. Mork thought that this action by Mindy was the most important thing he had found out so far about Earthlings. He sure had a lot to tell Orson in his next report.

***

15

When Tilwick drove up to Mindy's house, he was surprised that Mindy didn't even invite him in for coffee. In the first place she wanted to get Mork away from the policeman before he made things worse. And in the second place she needed to save all the coffee for Mork, who was famished for a hot pot of it and who gobbled up all the gardenias Mindy had bought for him.

Meanwhile, Tilwick wasn't sure he had done the right thing, letting Mindy bring that weirdo home. So he went immediately to Fred's and told him Mork was back in Mindy's apartment.

When Fred heard that Mork wasn't really crazy, that he was a rock singer on his way to Hollywood, who had a wife and child back in New York, he was enraged and suspicious all over again. He made Tilwick drive him to Mindy's, raving all the way that the story made no sense. What kind of crazy way was that to go to Hollywood from New York? Fred said. And the fact that

Mork had a wife and baby made him staying at Mindy's all the more frightening to Fred. "I'm gonna get to the bottom of this," Fred swore to Tilwick as he got out of the car.

"I can't wait or go in with you," Tilwick said, "because I'm on duty. But if you need me, call in to the station and they'll radio me."

So Fred banged on Mindy's door. She had locked it this time. She had learned from the disaster last time when her father had walked in without warning. "Dad," Mindy said, "what are you doing here?"

"You expected me to take this lying down?" Fred said angrily, barging past Mindy.

Mork looked at Fred with surprise. "I thought humans lie down flat," Mork said.

"What are you doing here?" Fred yelled at Mork. "Why aren't you with your wife and baby?"

"Dad!" Mindy protested, closing the door.

"What's all this about Hollywood? I want the plain, unvarnished truth of what you and Mindy were doing here last night."

"We were sleeping," Mork said.

Fred couldn't believe Mork was being so brazen. "Don't you have the decency even to lie?"

"Daddy," Mindy said, "it's not like it seems. The only reason he stayed here is because—"

Fred stared at her, waiting. Mindy hesitated. "Well?" Fred said.

"I can't tell you. It's a secret."

Fred drew himself up threateningly. "We've never kept secrets from each other—like the time you and Bonnie Tilwick drank that bottle of wine. Even though you were only seven, you came right in and told me."

Mindy shook her head and smiled sarcastically.

"Not exactly. I came right in and threw up on you."

"You see?" Fred said, as if she had proved his point. "And some kids can't even *talk* to their parents. Now, I demand to know what's going on between you two!" Fred looked at Mindy pleadingly. "After all," he added pathetically, "I love you."

"Ah," Mork said, impressed. "That is nice. Why don't you tell him, Mindy?" Mork hopped on his feet to get a better view of Fred's bald head. "Anyone that bald can't be all bad." On Ork, baldness was considered a distinguished attribute, mostly because it meant that a thin film of dust could settle nicely on the bald spots.

Mindy sighed. "You mean, Mork, that after all he's done to you, you're willing to trust him?"

"What have I done to him?" Fred demanded.

"Oh, come on, Dad," Mindy said, also angry. "You got him thrown into jail for doing nothing more than staying over at my apartment."

Fred looked embarrassed. "I didn't do that. Tilwick—"

"No excuses," Mindy said. "Tilwick only did what he thought would please you."

"Mindy-Earthling," Mork said in his deep announcer's voice, "please do not quarrel because of me." Mork looked very unhappy to Mindy. In fact, he had rushed through his dinner of gardenias and coffee and was suffering from *cez-gekup*, an unpleasant form of indigestion.

Mindy sighed again. Well, she had to confide in someone. She needed help with Mork's defense at the sanity hearing. And, besides, it was her father's crazy suspicion that had started this trouble. And who knew what more trouble Fred would create if Mindy didn't relieve his worries? "All right," she said. "But first you must promise never to breathe a word of this to *anyone*."

Fred had no intention of keeping the secret if it was something that might endanger Mindy, but he promised, anyway. Sometimes, being a father is a very confusing moral problem. "Okay, I promise," he said.

Mindy smiled. This was the first time she was able to be totally honest about Mork. And how badly she had wanted to spring this wonderful surprise on someone! She had been bursting with the desire to tell. Imagine meeting a spaceman and not being able to tell anyone about it! "Mork," she said, very excited, and looked at Mork with wide eyes, "is from Ork—another planet."

Fred stared.

"It's somewhere out beyond the Milky Way. You see, I was on this date—"

Fred turned and headed for the door.

"Dad! Where are you going?"

"Really, Mindy," Fred said, looking at her with disappointed eyes, "is that the best lie you can come up with?"

"It's true! It's true!" Mindy said, hopping up and down. "Mork," she said, grabbing her father and pulling him back into the living room, "prove it to him."

"Cosmic shtick?" Mork asked. "Coming right up." Mork went to the kitchen and came back with a glass of water. He put his *bloink* in it and drank it rapidly, while saying, "Many *bleams* ago, Orkans realized how much time could be saved if one could talk and drink at the same time. Let's see an Earthling do this."

Fred was thrown for a moment, but he shook

it off. "This is some kind of a trick. You're not fooling me."

"Wait," Mork said. He rushed to the closet and brought out something. "Here," he said triumphantly. "These are color slides of Ork."

"Really?" Mindy said. She had wondered almost constantly what the planet must really look like.

Fred took them skeptically, looked for a moment, and then tossed them to the floor. "Those pictures are completely black," he said with disgust.

"Oh, no," Mindy said, remembering the trouble she had had over the passport photo.

"But that's the capital city," Mork said, shocked that Fred wasn't impressed.

"This is pathetic," Fred said. "You're not fooling me with this nonsense. I want the truth. You couldn't possibly be an alien. Everybody knows what space creatures look like."

"Really?" Mindy said sarcastically. "What do they look like?"

"They have huge, bald heads, and scales all over their bodies, and claws instead of hands."

"Ah! I didn't know the *Rewpops* had learned how to handle intergalactic travel. I must tell Orson."

"Well, one thing is for sure," Fred said, returning his daughter's amazed look, "space creatures are always green."

"Oh," Mork said, nodding his head, "you want the old cliché." He pointed his *bloink* at his face and said, "Like this? *Krizle!*" The room hummed and Mork's face turned bright green.

Fred's eyes got huge and his mouth opened. He wanted to scream.

Mork turned his finger off and slowly returned

to his normal color. "Whew!" he said. "It isn't easy being green. My *bloink* is almost blinking, it's so tired."

"Uh, uh, uh," Fred said, backing toward the door, "I see, so you're from Outer Space, huh? Well, my goodness, you certainly are a good-looking young man. Are you on vacation?" Fred was almost to the door, but Mindy, knowing what her father was up to, get there ahead of him. "Mindy," Fred whispered frantically, fighting for the doorknob, "are you crazy? He might be here to snatch a body or something. Let me get help."

Mork walked toward him.

"Ha! Ha!" Fred said nervously. "Just kidding, just kidding."

"Dad," Mindy said, "Mork is from an advanced civilization. They did away with violence ages ago."

Fred was horrified. "You poor thing. He's brainwashed you." Fred turned the doorknob and started opening the door.

"Mork!" Mindy yelled. "Freeze it!"

Mork pointed his finger reluctantly. When Fred tried to pull the door open, it wouldn't move. "Mindy," Mork said, "I hope I don't have to do this for long. It hurts like the *yowtz*." The *yowtz* is a purple bird that can be found in the dense, pitch-black Orkian forests. *Yowtzes*, when pregnant, bite into an Orkan's ear and won't let go until they deliver their young. They don't do any permanent damage, but it is rather painful.

"Daddy," Mindy said and pulled her father into the living room, "listen to me. I am not brainwashed. Mork is harmless. If he meant to do any harm, why would he have gone so peacefully with Tilwick?"

That impressed Fred. He was very shocked by

the whole situation and he slumped onto the couch to consider it.

"Mork," Mindy said, "tell my father why you were sent here."

"My commander, Orson, sent me here to learn about Earth culture. I am to live like an Earthling and report on your society."

"So you're a spy!" Fred said, upset once more.

"No, no, Daddy," Mindy said. "He's a cultural ambassador. Don't you understand that if the Orkans wanted to, they could conquer our planet in a minute?"

"*Nin, nin,* Mindy," Mork said. "It would take at least an hour."

"Well, then," Fred said doubtfully, "why don't they?"

"It is impossible for us to harm life," Mork explained. "Though I can do anything with my *bloink,*" he said, holding up his right index finger, "even if I willed it to kill you, the deepest part of my mind would contradict that order. No Orkan has killed for more than two *Krell.*"

"How long is that in Earth time?" Mindy asked.

"Five thousand years," Mork answered.

"Do you mean to tell me," Fred asked, "that even if I was pointing a gun at you and was going to fire it, you wouldn't stop me?"

"If I stopped you, it would be by destroying the gun."

"And if you couldn't, if you had to kill me, you wouldn't do anything?"

Mork shook his head. "It would be impossible for me."

Fred kept Mork busy explaining the complicated world of Ork for many hours. By the end of the evening, Fred still didn't like the idea of his daughter living with Mork, but he agreed that there wasn't any choice. When they all got to discussing how to handle the sanity hearing, they were stumped. Though Mork didn't understand why Mindy and Fred didn't think they could risk getting another psychiatrist to examine him, he was willing to follow their advice. The problem was, they didn't have any.

"We'll just have to try and discredit Dr. Litney's testimony," Mindy said after Mork described his interview with the doctor in full. Orkans have total recall, and Mork's account was exact. "After all," she said, "what does the doctor have? All Mork did was fit a square peg into a round hole."

"How do we explain that?" Fred complained. "It's impossible."

"It is quite possible, Earthling," Mork said.

"I mean, by our standards," Fred explained, not too thrilled by Mork's superior abilities. Fred wasn't pleased at all by the idea that humans weren't the most intelligent beings in the universe.

"We don't explain it," Mindy said, smiling. "Don't you see? We pretend it never happened. Then the doctor will look ridiculous. Since it's impossible to do, we just act like it never happened."

"Well, we can give it a try," Fred said skeptically. Before he left to go home, Fred said to Mork, "I don't suppose there's any chance that you might go back to Ork?"

"Dad!" Mindy said.

"Sorry," Fred said and left. But his words didn't leave Mork's mind. When Mindy went to bed, Mork thought about all the trouble he had caused her. And, apparently, he was still going to cause her problems. She would have to defend him against the authorities, a very frightening thought to an Orkan, because Orkans never defy authority.

Yet, despite Mork's exhausting day (he could hardly lift his *bloink* an inch), he stayed up thinking about how wrong it was to endanger Mindy. Before she had gone to bed, Mork had asked her if what they had done with the passport was illegal on Earth. Mindy casually answered that it was—indeed, that it was a serious crime. She was rather excited by the notion that she had acted so boldly, though she was still quite worried about being found out at the hearing. But Mork was appalled that Mindy had taken such a chance for his sake. Though Mork had no qualms about breaking an Earth law, he felt it was wrong for him to encourage Mindy to do so. Besides, he shuddered at the thought of her being locked up. Orkans, it must be remembered, are forbidden to harm living things, even indirectly.

But it was late and time for bed. He'd worry about all this in the morning.

*** *** ***

16

Mork woke up the next day after dreaming about his life as an Orkling, and how Mindy would have loved it. Then he thought of Mindy and realized he was the cause of her troubles. He found a piece of paper and wrote her a note:

Mindy, I know you are willing to go on trying to help me, but I cannot allow you to harm yourself by breaking Earth laws, primitive though they may be. Do not worry about me. I have learned enough from you to be able to act like a real Earthling. Perhaps, when the Smokies are no longer interested in me, I will return. *Na-No, Na-No.*

He put it on the pillow Mindy had given him for the couch and packed up his belongings and left her apartment. As he left the building, carrying his suitcase, a small black boy, about ten years old, began to follow him. He was carrying schoolbooks and was dressed very much like Mork, in overalls and a T-shirt, except that he also wore a blue cap low over his eyes. When Mork reached the end of the block, he looked in the various directions, trying to decide which way to go. The boy caught up to him there. "Hey, mah man," he said, "are you a friend of Mindy's?"

"That is correct," Mork answered, looking at the boy, surprised to meet a human who was almost a foot shorter than himself. "Are you a *munchkin*?" Mork asked, remembering such creatures from an Earth program.

"No, I'm a brother," the kid answēred.

"Indeed. Mindy did not tell me she had a brother."

The kid laughed. "Hey, that's pretty hip. You a boyfriend of hers?"

Mork considered the word. "I am not sure."

"Had a fight, huh? Well, if ya ask me, ya blew it. Mindy's a foxy chick. She's on the charts as number one, if ya ask me." The boy said "If ya ask me" in a tone that suggested no one ever did ask him. "My name's Eugene. Pretty square, right? You can call me Gene."

"I am Mork."

"Say what?"

"Mork."

"Mork, huh. That's kind of a funky name. Are you Jewish, or somethin'?"

Mork looked at Eugene for a long time without speaking. Then he began twisting the skin on his knuckle.

"What ya doin'?" Eugene asked.

"I am attempting to adjust my language function. Are you speaking French? Perhaps you are using one of the dead languages that I am not equipped for."

Eugene removed his cap and shook his head from side to side, staring at Mork's eyes. Mork bent down to stare back. When he got low enough, Eugene pulled at the skin under Mork's eyes and got on his tiptoes to see better. "Well, they ain't bloodshot. Man, I don't know what you're on, but it's strong stuff."

"This is concrete," Mork answered, stamping his foot on the sidewalk pavement. "Fairly strong, but not nearly as sturdy as *fertz,* and it can't compare to *yoggle.*"

"Hey!" Eugene said and put out his hand. "Give me five, man."

"Five what?"

"Five fingers," Eugene said, slapping his own open palm to illustrate.

Mork slapped his hand as requested. "You are a hip dude," Gene said. "I'm sorry to hear that you and Mindy are splittin' up. I take lessons from her grandmother. Did you know that?"

Without waiting for an answer, Gene pointed to Mork's suitcase. "Are you goin' someplace?" he asked. "Are you takin' a vacation?"

"Well, in a sense," Mork answered. Since this was Mindy's brother, he was inclined to trust his judgment, despite Eugene's lack of stature. "Where would you go if you were taking a vacation?"

"Hmm." Gene put a finger to his chin. "Let's see. Well, I've always wanted to go to France."

"Okay," Mork said and began walking.

"I don't know, though," Gene said, hurrying after him. "I'd also like to see the Swiss Alps."

Mork stopped and turned to Gene. "Make up my mind. Which place?"

Gene was pleased by this question. Imagine an adult asking his advice! "Well," he said, trying to sound like an experienced traveler, "it depends on how much you got to spend."

Mork reached into his pocket, looking for the money that he had taken out of Mindy's purse. He had removed only a few of the smallest bills. He planned to return her money. "How much is this?" he asked Gene.

Gene looked at the bills. "Six dollars."

"So," Mork said, "then which place should I go to?"

"Six dollars! Is that all you got? You can't go to the Swiss Alps on six dollars."

Mork turned and began walking. "Then France it is."

"Hey! Hey!" Gene said, running after Mork and taking his arm. "You are really out of it, man. You can't go to France on six dollars."

Mork hung his head. "Oh, despair," he said. "Where can I go, then?"

"Man," Gene said, "you act like I did when I ran away from home."

"I am running away," Mork answered. "How could you tell?"

Gene pointed to Mork's face. "It's written all over your face."

Mork stepped back and began to touch his face with his hands, horrified. "It is? *Shazbot!* I've broken out in words!" Mork assumed this was a disease that infects people on Earth who are suffering from emotional exposure. "Listen," Mork pleaded, "my going away is a secret and I don't want you to tell Mindy where I'm going. I have been enough trouble to her."

"Man," Eugene said, "you ain't goin' far on six dollars. You can't even get a place to sleep for that—except in some flophouse."

It didn't seem to Mork that he could afford to be choosy, especially with all those words on his face, and the insanity people coming after him. "Where are these flophouses?"

"Well," Gene said, "there's some places on Mission Street, but they're awful seedy."

"That will not be a problem," Mork answered. "I am a trained horticulturalist. In which direction do I travel to find these flophouses?"

Eugene, being only ten, had only a dim notion of how to go, but he knew the general direction. He pointed the way and said, "Take care of yourself, brother. I hope you come back sometime. You're a cool dude." Gene put out his palm.

Mork slapped it and said, "Good-bye, *munchkin*." And he walked off, impressed that Mindy's brother had accepted him as a family member so quickly. These humans certainly are riotously emotional, he thought. But who could blame them, living on a planet with so many troubling things, such as this word disease? Mork pointed his finger at his face and put it on the washing mode, used by Orkans the way we humans use soap and water to clean ourselves.

***
17

Gene had directed Mork through the business district, and Mork reached it during rush hour. All those cars and people frightened Mork a bit. Orkans dislike crowds, which to them is any group larger than five persons. So, Mork hid in a park and watched until the traffic settled down. While he was there, something caught his attention that the television box had never shown. It was the strange religious worship by the creatures humans call dogs. Orkans have a different name for them. Mork wasn't sure that what he saw was a religious ritual; perhaps it was military. And the part humans played in it seemed to him ridiculous. He noticed it three times, and on the third occasion Mork decided to follow the human and the dog that had just taken part.

But first he had to inspect the temple of the dog's idolatry, those squat, red objects, with knobs on the sides. These red dog leaders, as Mork called them, must have special powers, because although Earth vehicles were parked in front of every other kind of object, they were not in front of the red dog leaders.

Mork went up to one and spoke with it. "I am Mork," he said. "I am not familiar with your customs, but I should like to learn. Could you explain why the dogs salute you as they pass?"

Mork didn't get an answer from the fire hydrant, so he bent down closer and tried to adjust the language function on his *bloink*. When he did, he began to sniff, with his finger, of course. Peculiar odor, he thought.

He tried many different languages, including Swahili, but the red dog leader didn't respond to any of them. Mork was about to try languages from other planets when he noticed that two or three humans were watching him. They seemed to consider his behavior unusual.

Mork was aware that he had to behave humanly, being a fugitive from a sanity hearing, and apparently he was committing some sort of sacrilege by bending down and talking with the red dog leader. So he had to relieve the minds of these humans who had begun watching. Mork stood up, turned to his side, and lifted his leg, saluting the red dog leader. "Quite a peculiar religion," he said aloud to himself as he walked quickly away.

He had taken so long at the fire hydrant that he had lost sight of the human and dog he had observed and decided to follow. But as he continued his walk to the flophouses Gene had recommended, he saw another pair practicing their faith at yet another red dog leader. How devout these humans are, Mork thought. He walked up to the human and said, "Pardon me, I am Mork. I .m a stranger here and I wonder if you could explain to me the meaning of this—"

At that moment, the human's dog lifted its leg. From the park Mork hadn't noticed this occur the other times. You see, in daylight Orkans have a little trouble seeing for distance. Mork had stopped speaking in astonishment. "Are you lost?" the human asked.

"No. I am Mork. I understand now. Please go on," he said to the dog, which had stopped and was looking curiously at this stranger and wagging its tail pleasantly.

The dog barked tentatively and its owner pulled slightly at the leash.

"Nice to meet you, too," Mork said to the dog. "Good-bye," he said to the human. Mork walked off, leaving the human to stare after him.

It wasn't much longer before Mork reached the area Gene had told him about. Mork had no idea that he was in the right location, nor that the place would seem unpleasant and scary to a human being. It was a skid row, full of drunks and bums and shady characters who used the area to hide stolen goods or beat up people with whom they were displeased.

Many buildings were deserted, the windows boarded up, or sometimes just with a few pieces of jagged broken glass left in them, or, sometimes, just wide open and empty. There were storefronts with nothing in them except one lone chair, and there were small grocery stores whose shelves were half-empty. The only clean establishment was a liquor store. The streets were filthy, the gutters littered with broken bottles and paper. Oh, Mork thought, what a pretty residential area. Indeed, it bore some resemblance to the most exclusive section of Ork's capital, the city of Kork.

Mork could not find any of these places called

flophouses that Gene spoke of, and he wandered in confusion. He was surprised that Gene thought he could find an inexpensive place to sleep in such a fine area, but he had to trust the boy he thought was Mindy's brother. He was about to give up, however, when he noticed one storefront, its window painted in a swirl of colors, that had a big sign reading: FRIENDS OF VENUS.

Mork was delighted and surprised. He went into the cold, long room that extended all the way to the back of the building. The room was beautifully decorated, from an Orkan's point of view. There were lots of spiders and plenty of dust. The walls were covered by writing, saying things like, ENNIS FROM VENUS SLEPT HERE, or, MARTIANS ARE NON-BELIEVERS, or, IF YOU'RE ON MERCURY, CALL 955-3131 AND ASK FOR MARY.

Toward the back were a few folding chairs facing a narrow cot. A man in a long white robe, with a few food stains, was standing in front of the cot speaking to no one.

"I told you *never* to sit on my throne," he said to the empty cot. "I leave you guys alone for five minutes and the whole place goes to pot. You scoff," he said with passion, spitting his words, "you non-believers. You don't believe the men from Venus are coming down to take us to their planet next Labor Day." The man, who was fairly short and had long, black greasy hair, raised his arms dramatically. "Then they destroy the Earth.

"And you!" he said, pointing an accusing finger at some invisible person on the cot. "You sit there eating a sandwich!" He was silent for a moment. "What? What's the passenger count now? Well" —he walked to a folding table and glanced at a clipboard—"so far we've signed up three. Oh," he sighed, rubbing his forehead wearily, "it's so hard getting recruits." The man slumped onto the cot and stared despairingly at the floor. "Oh, the pressure of it all. I've been walking the streets all morning trying to find believers, and what do I get for it?" He reached for his boots. "Sore feet," he said, pulling at his boots.

Mork felt sorry for this perceptive Earthling. After all, he understood how difficult it was to convince Earthlings that life existed on other planets. "Hello," Mork called out. "I am Mork," he said, walking toward the defeated figure on the cot who looked at him wearily, unsurprised by Mork's entrance. "I saw your sign, 'Friends of Venus,' outside, and I thought I'd drop in on the off chance that I might run into someone I know."

"I am Exidor," the man said, brightening at Mork's words. He hesitated as he asked this question, afraid that he was being teased. "You know some of the Friends of Venus?"

"*Nin, nin*," Mork said. "I only know some people from Venus. I got to know one very well. Cute —if you like short and fuzzy. His name was—" And Mork sneezed violently.

"God bless you," Exidor said.

Mork didn't understand why Exidor wanted that invisible Earthling to bless him, whatever that meant. "Oh, is that whom you were speaking to earlier? Anyway"—and Mork sneezed violently again—"had an adorable wife and a cute litter. Let's see, their names were—" And Mork spat, then made a beautiful ringing bell sound with his finger, followed by a buzz. And then he opened his mouth and out came a sound like thousands of people cheering at a sports event. "Poor child," Mork went on, "imagine being stuck with a name like—" And he made the sound of a crowd cheering again.

Exidor stood up, his eyes dancing with excitement. He held out his arms toward the ceiling and cried out, "A believer! A true believer!"

Mork shrugged his shoulders. "What's not to believe?"

"You believe in people from Outer Space?" Exidor said, still having trouble accepting Mork at face value. He had been tricked so often before, he was determined not to be toyed with by yet another jokester.

Mork was amazed by the perversity of human logic. Of course he believed in people from Outer Space; otherwise, all these Earthlings would have to be figments of his imagination. And why wouldn't humans believe in Venusians? Venusians, or *Mogglians*, as Orkans call them, look almost exactly like the human species called the dog. That was why Mork had assumed fire hydrants had to be more than public toilets. He was accustomed to thinking of dogs as having developed intellects. "Am I not myself from Outer Space," Mork said to Exidor, "when I land to visit my friends the Venusians?"

"Precisely!" Exidor was deeply impressed by this brilliant piece of logic. He jotted it down on his clipboard. "Please, won't you join me?" he asked Mork, getting out a Friends of Venus membership card.

Mork was taken aback. That was quite a rapid assumption of friendship, he thought to himself. But no doubt this poor fellow was lonely here on Earth. "All right," Mork said, "but not for long. Where would you like to be joined? At the elbow, perhaps? Or would you prefer the knee?"

"No, no," Exidor said. "I want you to join our group—become one of the Friends of Venus."

"Ah. I would like that very much. I am fond of the Venusians. But right now my task is to find something called a flophouse. I hope I won't have to go as far as Venus to find one."

Exidor laughed. Mork was surprised to hear a human's laugh sound so much like his own. "Well, you don't have to worry about flophouses anymore," Exidor said, waving his hand to show off his storefront. "You can stay here." Exidor turned to the cot and raised his arms. "You will work with us and we will triumph. I knew I would find someone. You came just as I had begun to despair."

"Work?" Mork said, remembering how worried Mindy was about him working. "You mean I've found a job and a place to flop out all at once? Lucky me. Mindy would be proud." Mork thought of Mindy. "Heavy sigh," he said. "Well," he went on, tossing something invisible with his hand, "must cast off gloomy thoughts, as you humans say. What do I have to do to apply?"

"Nothing," Exidor said, opening his arms generously. "Just believe." He closed his eyes reverently and then opened them quickly. "And give me all your Earthly possessions."

"That is a reasonable arrangement," Mork said, glad that he wouldn't have to part with any of his Orkian clothing: all those wonderful overalls and yellow T-shirts. "I haven't been here long enough to gather many possessions. I have only six dollars," he said, handing the crumpled bills to Exidor. "And a mosquito bite," Mork continued, offering his left forearm, which had, indeed, a large red lump on it.

"I don't want your mosquito bite," Exidor snapped.

Mork was disappointed. "Would you like to scratch it?" he suggested, thinking that might be valuable to an Earthling.

Exidor wasn't paying attention, however. He was greedily hiding Mork's six dollars somewhere inside his robe. "I can't tell you," Exidor said wildly, feverish with excitement, "how happy I am to meet someone who's actually seen Venusians."

Mork was surprised. "You have never seen them?" Mork was impressed that Earthlings were intelligent enough to believe in things that can't be seen. It is one of the first Orkian principles of intelligence.

"No," Exidor answered, his eyes looking into the distance. His hands trembled. "But I have heard them in my sleep. I know they are real and that they are our friends."

"Indeed," Mork said. "They are your best friends."

"Tell me!" Exidor grabbed his arm and squeezed hard. "Tell me everything you know about them! Here, sit on my throne," he said, pointing to the cot, covered by a dirty, threadbare gray blanket. Exidor waved at invisible people near the cot. "Get off! Get off!" he yelled angrily. "I want this true believer to sit on the throne—not you infidels!"

Mork was saddened. "I didn't know that you Earthlings had made the same mistake we did. Those poor people," Mork said, meaning what he thought were the victims of invisible experiments on Earth.

"Tell me!" Exidor said, his face reddening as he whispered intently. "What are they like?"

Mork sat on the cot. "Well, they're a good lot.

They walk on all fours and want to be everybody's best friend."

Exidor hugged himself, ecstatic. "I knew it! I knew it!"

"Oh, sometimes they get a little rowdy," Mork admitted. Orkans are always objective. "They love to bay at their moons and tip over garbage cans."

Exidor looked worried. "But that doesn't make them bad, does it?"

Mork shook his head. "*Nin, nin.* I prefer them to your dogs. At least they do not have an obsession with squat red objects."

"Listen," Exidor said, "I want to tell you my philosophy for the Friends of Venus." The crazed man got up and walked to his folding table, lifting a pamphlet. "Here, it is all in here," he said, still whispering intensely, as if the walls were his enemies. "I want you to study it. And then memorize it."

"Do I also have to eat it?" Mork said, knowing how Earthlings seemed to eat anything.

"No, no. We can burn it, instead. You must know so that we can convert people to our cause."

Mork took the pamphlet and said, "I'll study hard and let you know when I'm ready." Mork flipped the pages of the book with his left hand while he pointed his *bloink* at the pages as they went past. He looked up when he was done. It all took only a few seconds. "I am ready," he said.

Exidor was impressed. He leaned toward Mork, looking to his left and to his right to make sure that no one could overhear. "Did you learn that from the Venusians?"

"*Nin, nin,*" Mork said. "We monitored one of your Evelyn Wood speed-reading courses."

"You have memorized all that?" Exidor asked,

leering suspiciously. "You're ready to go out and convert others to our cause?"

"I believe I understand," Mork said modestly.

"All right, then. On your feet. We'll have a dry run. I'll be a non-believer and you try and convert me." Exidor ran to the other end of the store, almost tripping on his gown. Mork got up and tried to recall something from Earth television that would help him. He remembered seeing a preacher on Sunday morning.

"You!" Mork shouted. "You non-believer!" Exidor stopped and stared. "I have need of your attention. God has need of your attention, friend. Do you realize those Venusians are comin'?" Mork looked meaningfully at Exidor and let this sink in. "They are comin', all right. They are comin' here, not on Veteran's Day, not on April Fools' Day—but on Labor Day!" Mork lifted his arms to the sky and shouted, "Can you hear me? Are you ready? Because they're going to blow this planet to smithereens for our sins." Mork's voice echoed in the room, while he slowly lowered his eyes to glare threateningly at Exidor. "I see you are not laughing now—no, not now that you realize the day of Judgment is at hand. Is there no hope, you ask? Is there nothing that can be done for us miserable sinners?" Mork paused a moment and then smiled graciously, his voice suddenly soothing. "Well, my friends, it's not all bad news, because our friends the Venusians are sending a rocketship here to save *one* thousand of us." Mork's hand shot out as he yelled, "That's right! Not *two* thousand, not two *hundred* thousand, but *one* thousand—one thousand believers! Now, you can stay here. You can stay on this doomed planet and be without friends, without a home—yes, without even a planet beneath your feet. Or!" Mork's hands lifted to the sky. "Rise up with us and have a Venusian condominium of your very own!" Mork relaxed now and said in a normal tone, "Offer void where prohibited by law."

Exidor stood there, in the sudden silence, and looked at Mork with awe. "That's beautiful," he said quietly, a smile beginning to dawn on his scrunched-up, worried face. Exidor looked around him at the invisible people of his imagination and said, "Why can't you be more like him?" Exidor looked back at Mork and said again in a quiet, admiring voice, "That was superb."

Mork put his hands on his ears and twisted them like dials. "Na-No, Na-No," he said.

Exidor was very excited, his hands pulling nervously at his robe. "But you must tell me more about the Venusians you met on Earth."

Mork sat down on the cot. "Oh, I didn't meet them on Earth. I visited them on Venus."

Exidor stopped his nervous movements. "You—you mean you've actually been to Venus?"

"Oh, yes," Mork said casually. "I've visited every planet in this solar system."

Exidor's eyes bulged. "All of them?"

Mork waved his hand dismissively. "All except Pluto. It's a Mickey Mouse planet." Mork stood up. He had been considering this job offer and had come to a decision. "Exidor, as much as I need employment and appreciate your job offer, I must talk to you about your philosophy." Exidor nodded intently and Mork continued. "First of all, the Venusians aren't coming to Earth to blow it to smithereens."

Exidor cringed. So he had been fooled again, he thought bitterly to himself. He edged his way to the folding table, where he kept a long steak knife for occasions like this. He knew that those people from the hospital would come back for him, and he had no intention of letting them take him back to the mental hospital. This Mork had been clever, all right. "They're not?" Exidor said as he neared the table.

Mork said in a cheerful tone, "They don't even have the technology for space travel."

Exidor was almost there. He didn't want to move suddenly for it and tip off Mork. "They don't?" Exidor asked.

"Let us face facts," Mork said in a pleasant tone. He didn't want to be too hard on this Earthling. After all, at least Exidor knew there were other life-forms on other planets. "The most scientifically advanced invention of the Venusians is the garbage can. And they only developed that so they would have something to tip over. Necessity is the mother of invention."

Exidor had reached the knife. "Mork!" he yelled. "I had high hopes when you came in here. But you have tricked me. And for that you will die!" And he moved at Mork, waving his long knife.

* * *

18

Mindy had gone straight to the kitchen when she woke up and called out to Mork, asking if he wanted gladiolas or daisies for breakfast. When she got no answer, she went to rouse him, then found his note. She was terrified at the thought that he was out there wandering around. If he was taken in on another charge of nutty behavior, there would be no hope that they could get him through the hearing. And it was only ten minutes after she found his note when Deputy Tilwick phoned to ask if everything was all right. She had to reassure him three times because her first answer was so unconvincing. Tilwick said he would drop by around two o'clock to check on Mork, and when Mindy said that wouldn't be necessary, he asked once again if everything was all right, so she had to agree to be home at two.

Where would Mork go? she asked herself over and over. She thought about it and thought about it and noticed that time was passing, and that made her too nervous to think clearly, and so more time passed while she tried to calm herself down. At last, she realized she needed help, and the only safe person to see was her father.

She rushed to the store and found her father staring angrily at Cora's side of the store, which was full of customers, as usual, while his was almost empty. Mindy ran up to him and took him toward the back, while she whispered, "Daddy! Mork has run away. You've got to help me find him."

Fred couldn't help but be relieved that Mork had gone. "Honey, maybe it's for the best that he left. I mean, I don't know why he did, but—"

"He left to protect me! That's what's so awful about it. He felt bad that he had forced me to deceive the police." She looked at her father and didn't see what she hoped to. Fred looked as if he wouldn't help. "We have to find him," she pleaded. "He's like a child in our world. He has no concept of trouble or danger. If anything happened to him, I wouldn't be able to forgive myself."

Fred patted her gently. "Now, now, it's not your fault. Maybe he's right. Maybe it's better for you—"

"It isn't, Dad. Don't you realize that even running away won't help me? The police released him on my promises. He used my passport. If he doesn't show up for that hearing, they'll find out."

"Okay, okay," Fred said, convinced that he had to find Mork, at least for Mindy's sake. "I'll help you find him. But so what? Where do we look? He could have flown off anywhere."

Mindy sighed. "I don't know. But I don't think he went off in one of those Orkian flying Egg-Ships."

Fred let go of Mindy and snapped his fingers.

He looked excited. "You know, I thought that was strange."

"What?"

"You know little Eugene? He takes violin lessons here. Well, when he came in today, he said something about having met your new boyfriend."

Mindy tried to think if she had introduced Eugene to any of her dates. She hadn't. "You think he meant Mork?"

"Well, he took his lesson this morning before school. That meant he would have been walking past your apartment early in the morning."

"And he hasn't met Mork as far as I know," Mindy said, putting it together. "So you think he ran into him this morning when Mork was leaving?"

Fred shrugged his shoulders. "It's our only hope, right? We can't look all over town."

"Okay, let's go. We'll get Eugene at school." Mindy had a little trouble convincing Fred that they couldn't afford to wait until school let out. When Mindy said that they had to get Mork before two o'clock because of Tilwick, Fred claimed he could stall him. But she won Fred over by saying that the earlier they began looking for Mork, the easier it would be to catch up to him.

But Fred's worry about rushing into a school and asking to speak to a student was well founded. The secretary in the administrative office was all set to allow it until she discovered that Fred and Mindy weren't related to Eugene. She said in that case it was impossible, and when Mindy demanded to know why, the woman asked what it was they wanted from Eugene. That stumped Mindy. She began to mumble something about a valuable musical instrument, and the secretary said, "Are you accusing this pupil of theft?"

It was here that Fred showed his experience as a parent. He insisted that the secretary allow them to speak with the principal. He was told that the request was impossible because the principal was away for a school board meeting. Fred asked for the assistant principal, instead, and he was told they would have to wait for a half-hour.

Mindy almost went out of her mind pacing the hallway for what turned out to be a forty-five-minute wait. She was tempted to run upstairs to the classrooms and search for Eugene, but she realized that would lead to disaster. They would probably be thrown out. Meanwhile, Fred tried to think of a story to tell the assistant principal, and by the time that official arrived, he had a story ready.

Fred said that while Eugene had been taking his lesson that morning, Fred had also been looking over some musical arrangements he had been doing for a local quartet. Fred said he had lost the sheet music and he thought it might have gotten mixed up with Eugene's papers. The quartet needed the arrangement by this afternoon to rehearse for a performance tonight, Fred said, and he wanted to check with Eugene about it. The assistant principal agreed and gave Fred a note explaining the situation to Eugene's teacher.

Armed with the note, Fred and Mindy walked to Eugene's classroom and got the teacher to agree to let them talk with Eugene outside the class. By the time they had gotten the worried Eugene alone, more than an hour had gone by. Everything was going much too slowly, Mindy thought, as she said, "Eugene, don't be scared. But we were wondering if you met a young man named Mork outside my apartment this morning."

"I don't know nothin'," Eugene said. "I'm innocent!"

Fred smiled at Mindy. "I think we may have found a clue."

"Gene," Mindy pleaded, "this is very serious. Now, you did see Mork today, didn't you?"

Gene looked down at the ground and mumbled, "I thought you two split up." Suddenly Gene became bold. "What's wrong with goin' out with him? He's cool!"

Fred frowned, but Mindy smiled and put her arms around Gene, "I want him back, Gene. That's why it's so important for you to tell me what he said to you."

Gene was embarrassed. "I've been sworn to secrecy," he said.

"But Mork may be in danger. If you're his friend, what's more important—to keep your word to him, or to help him out if he's in trouble?"

Gene looked at her suspiciously. "What kinda trouble is he in?"

"Well," Mindy said patiently, "if he isn't back at my apartment by two o'clock, the police will arrest him."

Gene's eyes widened. "I'll tell ya," he said. "I don't know if he took my advice, but since he had only six dollars, I told him about the flophouses on Mission Street."

"Oh, no," Mindy said. "That's a weird neighborhood. He won't stand a chance there."

"On the other hand," Fred said sarcastically, "he might fit right in."

"Thank you, Gene," Mindy said, kissing him.

"Yecch!" Gene said. "But don't tell him I copped

a plea," he called out after Fred and Mindy as they rushed out.

While Fred drove to Mission Street, Mindy imagined all the horrible things that could have happened to Mork. They would kill a man for six dollars down there, she thought to herself, not to mention how quickly the police might arrest someone behaving oddly while there.

* * *

19

It was almost one o'clock when they arrived at Mission Street. Mindy suggested they split up to quicken the search, but Fred wouldn't agree. He didn't want Mindy walking alone there, even in broad daylight. They walked the length of Mission Street and saw no sign of Mork. Mindy felt depressed. She had expected, once Gene told them about his advice to Mork, that they would spot him immediately. Fred said that it was getting close to two o'clock and maybe they should go back to Mindy's apartment to meet Tilwick. They could confide in him, Fred suggested, and he would help with the search. Mindy violently refused. "Let's try this street," she said, pointing down an alley.

"All right," Fred said. "But then we've gotta head back."

About halfway down the block, Mindy excitedly pulled at Fred's arm. "Look!" she said, pointing to a glass window painted in a swirl of colors, with a sign saying: FRIENDS OF VENUS.

"Of course!" Fred said. "Let's go!"

They opened the door slowly, Mindy almost afraid to look, afraid that she might see Mork dead on the floor. At first, as they opened the door, they heard a man crying, moaning, and crying. "Forgive me! O! Forgive me, Venusian!"

That made Mindy swing the door open and run in. She stood there, stunned, at this sight. Mork stood in front of the cot with Exidor's steak knife in his hands, while Exidor was on his knees at Mork's feet, begging his forgiveness. Mork was poking his hand with the blade of the knife, watching it bend back on contact.

"Mork!" Mindy cried out, relieved. "You're all right?"

"Ah," Mork said, in a quiet tone from an Earthling's point of view, but in an ecstatic tone for an Orkan. "Mindy, it is good to see you. I find these Earth games very tiring. And I have made some sort of mistake."

"Pay heed!" Exidor cried out. "He has come! On your knees, infidels!"

Mindy looked at Exidor with disgust. "Why is he at your feet?" she asked Mork. Fred was behind her, unwilling to enter the filthy room.

"This is one of your, what I believe you call, astronauts. And he attempted some sort of probe into my body with this," Mork said, holding up the steak knife. "Apparently his knowledge of anatomy is limited," Mork went on, "because if I had allowed him to place this in my chest, as he planned, I'm afraid there would have been serious damage to my system. Why, I might have required as much as two weeks' rest."

"He tried to kill you?" Fred said, backing even farther out of the room.

"Ah!" Mork's finger went up in the air. "Was

that it?" Mork looked down at Exidor, still on his knees, hugging Mork's feet.

"He tried to kill you with a rubber knife?" Mindy asked.

"*Nin, nin,*" Mork answered. "Exhausted as I was, I decided it was worth the effort to prevent his probe, so I used my *bloink* to change this implement from steel to rubber. Plastic would have taken too much energy."

Mindy stared at the lunatic Exidor, whose eyes looked wildly at her and Fred. "He is the true one!" Exidor shouted at her. "Beware!"

"Mork," Mindy said, "let's get out of here."

Mork nodded. "I agree, Mindy-Earthling." He looked down at Exidor. "I am sorry, my friend, but I fear you have a bit to learn about intergalactic relations before landing on Venus," Mork said, extricating his feet from Exidor's passionate grasp. "Perhaps you might try a career as a medical technician," Mork said as he quickly hurried out after Mindy and Fred, while Exidor crawled after him, shouting, "Do not forsake me, O great Venusian! Take me from this doomed planet!"

"In a career as a medical technician," Mork said as he left, quoting one of those brief television shows called commercials, "you not only will have job security, but you can also help save lives."

They had to break into a trot in order to get away from Exidor, who followed them outside, pleading with Mork not to leave him behind. Once in the car, Mindy said to Mork, "Why did you leave? Don't you realize how much trouble you could have gotten into?"

"It is against our laws to hurt people," Mork explained. "I was causing you to risk jail, and also I was making your parental unit unhappy."

"Parental unit?" Fred mumbled. "I think, Mork, that we should be on a first-name basis. Just call me Fred."

"Mork," Mindy said, "it is very difficult not to cause human beings trouble if you know them," she said, looking meaningfully at her father. "You mustn't worry so much about whether you are causing trouble. Concentrate more on preparing for the sanity hearing."

"Well," Mork said, "how can I do that? There seems to be a great variety of acceptable human behavior." Indeed, this was one of the things that most puzzled Mork about Earthlings. On Ork, everyone's behavior was strictly defined. Either something was legal or it was not. On Earth, *munchkins* spoke differently from Mindy, Smokies talked like cowboys, Fred spoke like the daddy on "Father Knows Best," and Cora spoke like nobody Mork had ever heard. It was all very confusing.

***

20

Mindy tried to explain to Mork about Earth behavior as they hurriedly went back to her apartment. They were still talking when they got to her apartment, where they found Tilwick, waiting impatiently. "I sure am glad to see you," he said. "I was just about to call in that Mork had run off."

"Away," Mork corrected.

"What?" Tilwick said, alarmed.

"Nothing," Mindy snapped. "Everything's fine."

"Well, his lawyer is here," Tilwick said, standing aside to reveal a shy, pale, brown-haired young man who was carrying a huge folder of papers. The papers were slipping out the sides of the folder and the young man had trouble pushing them back in.

"Hello," he said, his eyes on his papers. "My name is George Hendley. The court appointed me."

"Greetings," Mork said pleasantly.

Mindy pushed Mork on into the building. "Uh,

he doesn't need a lawyer," she said, turning and blocking Hendley's way in.

Tilwick frowned. "Don't be silly, Mindy. That's exactly what he does need."

"Well, we'll hire one," Mindy answered defensively.

"We will?" Fred said, thinking of his low bank balance.

Hendley cleared his throat and a paper fell to the ground. "Pardon me," he said. "Until you do hire another lawyer, it is my responsibility to interview, uh"—George turned his head to look at a paper he was holding on top of the folder—"Mr. Mork Ricardo, in case, for some reason, he appears without legal representation."

Tilwick looked at Mindy suspiciously and she realized that she had to let Hendley interview Mork, or Tilwick would start asking questions she didn't have any answers for. Besides, this Hendley didn't seem to be bright enough to figure Mork out. Maybe nobody was, she decided. "Okay," she said, letting Hendley in. "I'll see you later, Dad."

Tilwick and Fred left reluctantly and Mindy let Mork and George into the apartment. "Sit down on the couch, Mr. Hendley," she said, pulling Mork aside. "Be careful," she whispered to Mork.

Mork nodded solemnly and tiptoed into the living room. George was too busy shuffling papers to notice the super-cautious way that Mork walked into the room. "Um, now, let's see, Mr. Ricardo, you have a wife named Lucille?"

"Sí."

"You don't speak English?"

"I don't?" Mork said. He was astonished by this news. He looked down at the knuckle of his *bloink* and turned it a notch. "*Pardonnez-moi,*" Mork said in perfect French, thinking, however, that he had adjusted his language mode to English.

Mindy knew immediately what was happening. Mork had explained the language device installed in his *bloink*. It was a special machine that allowed Mork to speak any language. All he had to do was set the right dial. "It conjugates, it punctuates, it can do idioms—even most slang!" Mork had told her this, adding, "Only two *brandels* and your money back if not satisfied."

"Uh, Mork," she said, "when you said '*Si*' to Mr. Hendley, he thought, since that is the Spanish 'yes,' that you don't speak English. But you had been speaking perfect English up to then."

Mork nodded and turned his knuckle back to the English mode. Meanwhile, George was staring at Mindy. "Are you a law student?" he asked with a worried look.

"Me?" Mindy said, surprised. "No."

"So you do speak English?" George asked Mork.

"I can speak any language you wish," Mork said, trying to be friendly. "If you're not comfortable with English, we can try Russian."

Mindy laughed in a fake, high-pitched way. "What a kidder," she said.

George didn't find the joke funny. "Yes, apparently it's all this kidding that has gotten you into this mess." He rustled some more papers. "Your wife is not available for the hearing?" he asked Mork.

"Lucy is available to the hearing and to the sighted. She is very generous to all the charities," Mork answered, remembering many humans had said so on those programs where you sat in the home of Here's Johnny and Johnny's friend whose stomach kept getting smaller as the years went by.

"Mr. Ricardo!" George said huffily, his fingers pushing his glasses back nervously. "If you do not start taking this situation seriously, you will find yourself in a straitjacket."

This disturbed Mork. He didn't want to have to wear anything except his overalls. "I am most apologetic," he said, hoping this would prevent any jacket-wearing. After all, he still wasn't sure which way jackets were supposed to be put on.

"Now, I will ask you again. Can your wife appear in your defense?"

"No," Mindy answered quickly. "She has to remain in New York."

"Hmm," George said. "That's a pity. Are these friends, the Mertzes, available for testimony?"

"No." Mindy jumped in again before Mork could speak. "But I can testify for Mork. And so can my father."

"How long have you known Mr. Ricardo?" George asked.

"Well," Mindy said, then paused, wondering if she could get away with a lie.

"My information here is that Mr. Ricardo lives in New York and is only here in Boulder because he is in transit to, uh, uh"—George looked up, surprised—"Hollywood?"

"I'm up for a part in a big new motion picture!" Mork said happily.

"I'm afraid," Mindy said quickly, "that I've only known Mork for a few days. But he is the most sane person I know," she insisted and meant it. "He's eccentric, I admit, but that's not against the law."

"Well, I imagine," Mr. Hendley said, "that as a

Cuban, some of your traditional cultural manner-
isms might be misunderstood. And as for these I.Q.
tests, it has been proved that they are culturally
biased." George hunched over his papers again
and then exclaimed. "What? How is that possible?" George looked at Mork. "How did you fit a
square peg into a round hole?"

"He didn't," Mindy said.

"Well, the psychiatrist's report says that he did."

Mork shrugged his shoulders. "Dumb luck?" he
suggested.

George shook his head as he continued to read
Dr. Litney's report. "The best thing we can do is
to have Mr. Ricardo examined by another psychiatrist, so that we can get a contradictory opinion."

Mindy violently opposed this idea. Mr. Hendley
challenged her to give a reason why they shouldn't.
Was she afraid that another doctor would confirm
Litney's opinion? he asked.

"I think," she said, "that many doctors would
find Mork's Latin habits to be strange, as you said.
I don't think we could find an impartial psychiatrist."

George considered this. "Do you think we should
try and defend Mr. Ricardo as a political prisoner?"

"You mean," Mork interrupted, "that there
would be demonstrations?" He had seen such
things on those programs where Earthlings sit at
desks, smiling while they show pictures of people
being killed and buildings burning down. " 'FREE
MORK' signs?" he went on, intrigued by the notion.

George stared at Mork. He had heard that
Cubans were a carefree people, but this complete
lack of concern that Mork showed for his own
freedom was disturbing. "I think," Mindy said loud-

ly to stop Mork from talking, "that we should con-
sult another lawyer." She stood up. "Mork is tired,
Mr. Hendley. I'd like you to leave."

George got up, papers fanning out from his
folder, and he tried to squash them back in while
speaking angrily. "Ms. McConnell, I think that if
you do not allow me to get all the facts, Mr.
Ricardo is going to be in hot water at that hearing."

"*Shazbot!*" Mork cried out. "My skin will look
like Prune City!"

"I think it's all a language problem," George said,
while Mindy took his arm and urged him to the
door.

"Good-bye," Mindy said as she opened the door
and gave George a gentle shove out.

Mork was busy inspecting the unit in his knuckle. "I think I will ask for my money back," he
said, dismayed that all his troubles were apparently due to a failure of Orkian technology. But as he
considered the lawyer's theory—that all of his
problems were due to language difficulties—he realized that it must be so. The language device
could only tell him the meaning of Earth words
out of the situation in which they were being used,
and Earth words change their meaning depending
on what words surround them. This, as has been
said, is not true of Orkian language. Each Orkian
word always means the same thing, no matter
what the situation. Orkans do not have expressions
like "You'll be in hot water," which means something different from what the words say.

If you say to an Orkan, "Go soak your head,"
he would immediately plunge his head into the
nearest body of water, especially since an Orkan
breathes with his fingers and he would have no
fear of drowning. Mork was convinced that all the

confusion and violence on Earth was due to this sloppy use of language. His problem was that he could not adjust his language device to function differently. Nor would he want to. From Mork's point of view, to learn how Earthlings misuse language would be as silly as a human trying to learn how to add incorrectly. Clarity and Legality are the words on the giant, dusty, spider-webbed arches that are the entrance to Kork, Ork's capital. Actually, the words printed there read: FRUX EEK PRUX, which mean Clarity and Legality in English. You see, there's the problem—in English they don't mean quite what they mean in Orkian.

Mindy, meanwhile, also wasn't feeling optimistic about Mork's chances in the courtroom. She had only that night to coach Mork in human behavior. Besides, even if she had a month, that wouldn't be enough. There were too many confusing things that might be said to Mork for Mindy to be able to think of them all. What amazed her was that no one seemed to think that blue-eyed Mork— with his Scandinavian features, speaking without a trace of a Spanish accent—was being accepted as a Cuban. She couldn't believe that no one had noticed that Mork was using all the names from the "I Love Lucy" television show. Yes, no matter how childish and naïve Mork seemed to her, her own people, human beings, seemed even more ridiculous.

* * *

21

Mindy spent most of the night preparing Mork for the hearing. She told him that he should pretend he was kidding the psychiatrist, and that he should apologize for doing so. Also, she told him that he shouldn't use the "I Love Lucy" show for any more facts if he was asked anything else about his wife and son.

Fred called after work and asked if he could help. He also wanted to sleep over, but Mindy told him neither was necessary. Mindy was able to convince Mork to try sleeping on the couch one more night, and she explained at great length why she was helping him. Mork had a lot of trouble understanding why Mindy would risk jail for him, and he still seemed to disapprove, even after Mindy had told him it was a natural human emotion.

"I feel badly for you primitive Earthlings," Mork said when she was finished. "But it is good that you aid me. Orson will be pleased when I report to him."

The next morning, Tilwick came by with Fred

and picked up Mork and Mindy to drive them to the hearing. It was held in a judge's chambers, with only the judge, a prosecutor, a court reporter, Tilwick, Dr. Litney, George Hendley, Fred, Mindy, and, of course, Mork, present.

The prosecuting attorney was a man in his forties, a fat man with bushy gray and black hair, who wore thick black glasses that made his eyes look large. The judge was thin, in his sixties, almost completely bald, and he spoke softly and compassionately. Hendley came up to Mork and Mindy the moment they arrived. "Did you hire another lawyer?" he asked nervously.

"No. Mork won't need a lawyer," Mindy said.

"The court will insist that I represent him," Hendley said. "Look, let me defend him. I'm sure I can convince the judge that this is all due to the language problem."

Mork looked down at his knuckle and said, "Perhaps he is right, Mindy. Let him have his chance."

The judge banged his gavel. "Are we ready?" he said in his quiet but commanding voice. Everyone sat themselves around the large table, with the judge at its head. There wasn't enough room for Mindy and Fred at the table, so they sat on a couch nearby. "All right," the judge continued. "This is just an informal hearing. We will not be under strict courtroom procedure. Uh, Mr. Flount," the judge said, looking at the prosecutor, "will you begin?"

"Thank you, Your Honor. Let me summarize the reasons for this hearing. Mr. Mork Ricardo was encountered by Deputy Tilwick at the home of one Mindy McConnell. He found—"

"Objection," said Mr. Hendley, his voice suddenly squeaky.

The judge seemed irritated. "What are you objecting to?"

"Well, Your Honor," said Hendley, "I'd rather that the prosecutor just present evidence. I'm not willing to concede any facts until I hear someone testify to them."

"Your Honor," Mr. Flount began, looking fierce, "I am merely—"

The judge put up his hand. "Look, gentlemen, I don't know about you, but I don't want to spend a beautiful day like today inside. Now, I've said that this is informal, so can we just hurry this along? Mr. Flount, if you have witnesses, let's hear them."

Flount looked unhappy while Hendley smiled at Mindy, as if to say: See how good I am? "All right, Deputy Tilwick, could you tell us what—"

"Your Honor," Hendley piped up again, "isn't this man going to be sworn in?"

The judge frowned. "Mr. Hendley, I know you're a young lawyer so I'm going to forgive this zeal. This is not a courtroom, just a hearing. Deputy Tilwick knows that he is going on record and can be held accountable. Proceed, Mr. Flount."

"Deputy, could you tell us what happened when you met Mr. Ricardo?"

Tilwick had been worrying about this moment all night. His duty was to report what occurred, no matter how angry Mindy was at him for doing so. Still, he intended to soften his testimony, until he realized that he would look bad if it seemed that he had arrested Mork without cause. And from the looks of Hendley, Tilwick knew he had better show cause. "Well, I dropped by Ms. McConnell's and found Mr. Ricardo there. When I asked him where Mindy was, he said something about her being at work, and then he said that work was a strange idea."

"Could you just tell us what about his behavior seemed strange to you?" Flount said.

"Yes, sir. We were talking and suddenly he asked me if I was part of Space Patrol, and when I asked if he was putting me on, he said no, that I wasn't even hollow." The court reporter, a young woman, began to titter. "And then I sat down on a chair and there was an egg on it."

"A whole egg? Unbroken?"

"Yes, sir. Mr. Ricardo got very upset that I had sat on his egg, and he began speaking to that egg and to all the other eggs—"

"Other eggs?"

"Yes, sir. I then saw that there were lots of other eggs placed on the couch and chairs in the room. He began talking to them about why they didn't fly away, and so on."

"What did you do then?"

"I thought maybe he was on drugs, so I searched him and didn't find anything, but he started making weird noises. I asked him if he had any identification and he said no and made more noises. So I took him in on a John Doe and recommended that a psychiatrist see him."

"That's all," Flount said, a hand pointing to to Hendley.

"Uh"—Hendley was fiddling with papers—"Uh, Deputy Tilwick, do you speak Spanish?"

"Excuse me?" Tilwick said.

Hendley stared at him. "I asked if you speak Spanish, the native tongue of Mr. Ricardo."

"No, sir, I don't."

Hendley nodded vigorously, as if he had made a great point. "So these so-called strange noises that

Mr. Ricardo made while you were illegally searching him—"

"Your Honor," Flount moaned.

The judge leaned forward. "Mr. Hendley, again I will remind you that this is not a formal hearing. That sort of line should be saved for a more urgent and serious procedure. Could you just stick to the evidence dealing with Mr. Ricardo's competence?"

"Yes, Your Honor," Hendley said. "These strange noises, Deputy Tilwick, they might have been Spanish words, mightn't they?"

Tilwick looked unhappy. "Well," he mumbled, "they didn't sound like Spanish."

"I didn't ask you that," Hendley snapped. "I asked if they *could* have been Spanish."

"Yes, sir, I guess they could have."

"So you took Mr. Ricardo in because he placed eggs around a room and didn't have any identification. Now, he has identified himself to you, hasn't he?"

"Yes, sir."

"So your only complaint against him is that he talks to eggs?"

"Yes, sir."

"I don't have any other questions, and I move that this hearing be dismissed."

The judge snorted. "You can't dismiss a hearing. You adjourn it." This nicety of language impressed Mork. He had already been impressed by the judge's baldness, a mark of distinction on Ork. "Anyway, I believe we have to hear from Dr. Litney. Mr. Flount?"

"Thank you," Flount said, looking at Dr. Litney. "The court is well aware of your qualifications, Dr. Litney. Now, after you examined the defendant, what were your conclusions?"

"After extensive tests," Dr. Litney said, looking at Mork with distaste, "I concluded that the patient is extremely childlike and incapable of learning. I also found marked anti-social behavior, and therefore I believe that he isn't competent to function in society."

"Could you tell us what, in your tests, showed these tendencies?"

"Well, he was very defensive about the Rorschach cards. He refused to admit that they suggested any imagery, even after I explained the process to him. This usually indicates latent hostility and defensiveness and also an inability to learn. The same thing occurred on the word-association test, where he insisted on giving me commercial products in response to general words."

"For example?"

"Well, when I asked 'Woman,' he replied 'Chanel Number Five.'"

"Anything else?"

"Yes. On the standard wooden-blocks I.Q. test, he insisted on attempting to fit a square block into a circular hole, thereby destroying a perfectly good board." Dr. Litney looked upset at the idea of his board being destroyed.

"That's all." Mr. Flount gestured to Hendley.

"Dr. Litney," Hendley said, "when you asked for the defendant's name and address, he provided you with that information willingly, did he not?"

"Yes, he did."

"He told you that he had been raised in Cuba, an underdeveloped country, did he not?"

"Yes."

"And yet you gave him tests that are specifically designed for people who have been raised in a white, middle-class society?"

Dr. Litney sneered. "Mr. Hendley, these tests can be taken by anyone of any cultural background. They are simple requests to find pictures on cards smeared with ink, something anyone can do, and the blocks are a basic test of a person's ability to judge perspective. As for the word association, anyone knows what words like 'dog' and 'woman' mean."

Hendley looked dismayed. "But Mr. Ricardo is not as familiar with English as a native-born American would be. He answered you with television-advertised products because Mr. Ricardo learned English by watching television."

"Your Honor," Mr. Flount said, "is Mr. Hendley questioning Dr. Litney or debating with him?"

"I agree," the judge said. "These are basic tests which are recognized throughout the world. Language should not be a problem here. Dr. Litney says that Mr. Ricardo shows an inability to learn—"

"Your honor," Hendley said, "all I'm trying to show is that Mr. Ricardo deserves to be examined by a psychiatrist who is fluent in Spanish and can judge him on his—"

"I object!" Mindy yelled, jumping up from the couch.

Everyone turned and looked at Mindy with surprise. The judge looked at her with the trace of a smile. "Young lady, cases of this kind are not supposed to be a public spectacle."

"I'm here as a character witness for Mork. Your Honor, I'm Mindy McConnell, and this is my father. I want to go on record as saying that Mork has a right to *not* have a lawyer. I will not permit him to be put in a mental hospital because his lawyer doesn't know what he's doing."

The judge blinked and then rubbed his eyes. "Young lady, do I understand you correctly? You are objecting that Mr. Ricardo *does* have counsel?"

"That's right," Mindy said. She looked hopefully around the room and then burst out, saying, "Mork is innocent! True, he is a little different from most, but this great country was built on the rights of the individual to be individual. We have the God-given right to be eccentric, and therefore I demand that Mork be exonerated and set free!"

Fred began to applaud proudly, but the judge stared at him until he stopped. "I suggest," the judge said, looking at Mindy, "that you sit down."

Mindy was embarrassed. "I'm sorry," she mumbled.

"She's sorry," Fred explained.

The judge looked around the room and sighed. "Well, now that everything is back to normal, let me consider the suggestion made by the defense counsel—"

Mindy groaned and put her head in her hands. She knew that if Mork was examined by another psychiatrist, he would be found out. Mork, meanwhile, had been enjoying the proceedings. They were so much like the television dramas, except that no one seemed to be as good as Perry Mason. Things looked bad for him, he knew, so it was time for a surprise witness, or a brilliant cross-examination. Mork remembered an especially good drama he saw, *Inherit the Wind,* where Spencer Tracy, when all was lost, got up and conducted a wonderful questioning ritual. Mork got up and put his finger behind the straps of his overalls. "Your Honor," he said in a slow, wise voice.

"Yes, Mr. Ricardo?" the judge said, as surprised as everyone else that Mork was talking.

"If I correctly understand your law, I have a right to speak for myself?"

"Yes," the judge said. "This is informal, and a statement from you will be welcome."

"I was hoping," Mork said with a slight deferential bow, "that you would permit me to question Dr. Litney." Mork paused and the judge nodded his approval. Mork turned to the doctor. "Dr. Litney, is it true you don't like me?"

Dr. Litney looked irritated. "Your Honor," he protested, "I've never been interrogated by a patient before."

"Then how," Mork said triumphantly, "do you know I'm doing it now?"

The others in the room giggled. Even the judge smiled and then said, "Dr. Litney, in the interest of justice, why don't you answer Mr. Ricardo's questions?"

Mork began to pace as he asked in a booming voice, "You said I was anti-social. In what way?"

"Well"—Dr. Litney's voice was aggrieved—"you refused to cooperate. You wouldn't participate in my tests."

"You refused to answer my questions," Mork pointed out. "Does that make you anti-social?"

"It isn't my job to be interrogated by patients."

"It isn't my job to take your tests," Mork replied calmly. There was a murmur around the room. Mork's logic was impressive. For an Orkan, it was child's play. Remember, every Orkan is a trained lawyer. Although, on Ork, there are no jury trials, indeed there are no courts. Legal matters are settled by committees that communicate telepathically.

"Now," Mork said, running his fingers up and

down the suspenders of his overalls, "about the tests you ran that made you hate me—"

"Your Honor," Dr. Litney said, his voice breaking with frustration, "I don't hate the man, but, as I've said, in one of my tests he tried to fit a square peg into a round hole."

Mork raised his hand in triumph. "But I did it!"

Dr. Litney banged the table in frustration. "Yes! I don't know how you did it, but I *can't* get it out! You've ruined a perfectly good board. Do you know what those things cost?"

"And that's why you dislike me," Mork said, looking significantly at the audience. They were fascinated. Dr. Litney was breaking.

"I don't have time for this," Litney said, his hands grabbing nervously at his head.

Mork frowned. What did he mean? Mork wondered. He put his foot on the table and lifted his pants leg. There, on Mork's ankle, was a watch. Mork looked at it and said to the astonished room, "The time is ten-thirty-six."

"See!" Litney almost jumped up from his chair in excitement. "Do you see that? He wears his wristwatch on his ankle!"

Mork looked offended. He turned to the judge. "No, Your Honor, as anyone can plainly see, I wear an *ankle*watch on my ankle. If I wore an anklewatch on my wrist, now that would be crazy!"

Litney put his hands to the others. "He's a wiseacre! Your Honor, there's nothing he won't joke about!"

Mork bent down toward Litney and insinuated in a whisper, "And you don't like wiseacres, do you?"

"No!" Litney shouted. "I don't!"

"Aha!" Mork straightened up. "So you're prejudiced against me."

"I didn't say that!" Litney yelled, pointing to the court reporter. "Do you see how cleverly he's twisting my words? I didn't say that!"

"Oh!" Mork leaned back, smiling with wonder. "I see! I see! So now I'm clever. Isn't that another word for intelligent?"

"No!" Litney's hands reached for Mork, as if the doctor wanted to take back his previous statements. "No, it's not! It's not another word for intelligent; it's another word for wiseacre." Litney turned pleadingly to the judge. "Do you see how he's twisting my words? He's sneaky." Litney looked at the others hopefully, but they looked doubtful, surprised that Mork had reduced the doctor to wild pleading so quickly. "He's sneaky!" Litney cried. "On the inkblot test, for example, I asked him what he saw, and he said, 'It looks like somebody spilled ink.'" Litney picked up the card. "Anybody can plainly see what these two people are doing!"

Mork watched the others. They were shocked by the doctor's deterioration. "It seems," Mork said, in a quiet voice that sounded ominous, however, "that everything hinges on whether I am capable of learning."

"That's right," Litney agreed. "And you flunked the word-association test outright."

"You mean, when you would say a word like 'white'?"

"Yes, and you might say 'black.'"

"Tall?" Mork said in a clipped voice.

"Short."

"Sky?"

"Birds."

"Sex," Mork hissed.

"Pamela," Dr. Litney answered and then looked horrified. At the other end of the table, the court reporter, whose name was Pamela, jumped up, her face reddening.

"You promised you'd never tell! You said you'd never tell!" She began to weep and hurried out of the room, mumbling through her tears, "Never! Never!"

The prosecutor also rose to his feet. His face was hurt and he looked angrily at Litney. "You and Litney? Pamela," he called after her. "I thought we were—"

Dr. Litney, frightened, grabbed his papers and mumbed, "Your Honor, I have a patient to see—" And he ran out the door, shouting, "Pamela! Pamela!"

The prosecutor was also quick. "He's not going without me," he said. And he rushed out the door, also calling, "Pamela! Pamela!"

The judge looked at his room, with only Tilwick, Mork, Hendley, Fred, and Mindy left. Mork was the only person who seemed undisturbed by these events. "The defense rests," he said with a slight smile.

The judge sat for a moment in stunned silence. Then he got slowly to his feet and began to walk around the table, looking with shock at the empty chairs of the prosecutor, Dr. Litney, and Pamela. He cleared his throat. "Well, I think I had better make a ruling. Now, while it is true that the defendant, Mr. Ricardo, may add a new dimension to the word 'eccentric,' there is no law against that. And since it appears that he is no danger to himself or society"—the judge looked at the empty chairs—"and since we have no one to prosecute or testify or even to write down what I'm saying, let's just—oh, case dismissed!" The judge banged his gavel, and Mindy jumped in the air.

"Mork! You won!"

Hendley mumbled to himself, "We won?"

Mork put out his hand in the Orkian handshake to Hendley. "Well done. *Na-No, Na-No*." And Mork twisted his ears as if they were dials. Hendley just stared.

Mindy said in a rushed whisper to Mork, "Let's get out of here."

Mork looked disappointed. "Couldn't I do this as my job?" he said, while Mindy and Fred pulled him out of the building and into the beautiful sunny day.

"Let's celebrate," Mindy said while they walked to the car, but Fred insisted that they had to get back to the store.

"All right," Mindy agreed. "But can we go out to a fancy restaurant for lunch and have champagne?"

Mork hopped up and down excitedly. "Will Lawrence Welk be there?"

Mindy was so happy that everything had worked out that she didn't bother to explain Lawrence Welk wouldn't be in a Boulder restaurant. Indeed, she didn't bother to warn Mork about his behavior all day, not even when he played a record for a customer who mistook him for a salesman by putting his *bloink* down on the turntable instead of the needle.

It was a wonderful day! Fred agreed not to bother her about Mork living in her attic, and Mindy happily spent the evening cleaning it up for Mork. He watched her with horror as she vacuumed up all those webs, holding the spiders in his hands while he mumbled to them, "It's all right. Just think of it as a hurricane, and of me as the Red Cross."

* * *

22

That night, as all of Boulder, Colorado, slept, except perhaps for the lunatic Exidor, who still searched the skies for Venusians, Mork swung himself down from the rafter he had been hanging from and sat in the *UdFred* position. This was used by all Orkans for telepathic communication. Orson had ordered Mork to report to him once a week, and Mork thought that the events so far were worthy of discussion.

Mork held his *bloink* against his forehead while smoke trailed from its tip and he chanted, "*Jex, Bex, ekk Yex!*" for a few minutes. He was having trouble clearing intergalactic interference. "Those darned Martians," he mumbled, "always tinkering with the *Friboz* waves." He sent out a laser clearing beam and repeated his chant, finishing it by saying, "Come in, Orson. Come in, Laser Breath."

"Watch it, Mork!" Orson's voice boomed in his brain. "I'm only sixty million light-years away."

"I am sorry, great Orson, but those Martians get on my nerves."

187

"Mork!" Orson's voice was harsh. "Have those humans infected you already? You don't have any nerves." Orson sighed. His sigh was like the wind force of a cyclone. "Just tell me what you have learned of this primitive culture."

"Oh, I have learned a lot," Mork said proudly. "So much is hard to comprehend."

"I do not understand, Mork. How can a primitive society be difficult to understand?"

"Well, everyone on this planet is an individual."

"What?"

"Yes, and they are proud of it!"

"Amazing!" Orson's huge head rocked from side to side, clouds of dust rising from his head. "How can a society function if everyone's different?"

"Well, if someone gets *too* different, he is thrown into a place called the 'slammer.' " Mork sent Orson a telepathic picture of the jail cell he had been put in.

Orson frowned. "That is punishment? It seems a bit small, but rather nice."

"Not on Earth," Mork said. "Here, these awful places are considered pleasant." Mork sent Orson more pictures: of Mindy's apartment and of Fred's store.

Orson curled his lip. "How disgusting. No dust."

"Everything is very different. Indeed, I got into trouble because of these differences. They put me into the 'slammer.' "

"Hmm," Orson mumbled to himself. "Perhaps they *are* intelligent on Earth." Then he boomed at Mork, "Have you found a decent place to stay?"

Mork showed Orson a picture of Mindy's attic. "How about this? It's a cute studio, don't you think?"

"But Mork, where are the webs for all those spiders?"

Mork sent a picture of Mindy. "The Earth girl who saved me from the 'slammer' insisted on clearing them away."

"Is she hostile?" Orson asked, appalled by her clearing away the webs.

"No," Mork said, sending pictures of Mindy defending him at the hearing and in the jail. "That is what is so confusing. She came to my defense and defied the system, though she hardly knew me."

"Why would she do that?" Orson said, letting a spider run playfully up his arm. "Is she a clone?"

"No, no. On Earth this sort of thing occurs all the time. It has something to do with emotions."

Orson nodded and more dust trailed off his head. "Investigate this phenomenon closely. It is interesting behavior, even if it is irrational."

Mork suddenly sent another image, that of Exidor discussing the Venusians. "Look out for this Earthling," he said to Orson. "He is far ahead of the others, though, of course, still primitive. And also"—Mork sent images of Earth life compared to television—"our theory that the entertainment box is a fantasy world is completely wrong. It is a good guide to ordinary life."

Orson's voice sounded pleased. "That is a good discovery. Have you made contact with any of the television Earthlings?"

"Not yet, but I will try. I have much to do here. There are two diseases that must be cured. Humans speak of them fearfully: the common cold, and something called the Saturday Night Fever."

"Anything else?"

Mork sent another image of Mindy. "This may

sound strange, Orson, but knowing that some
body would risk her safety to defend me makes me
feel"—Mork searched for the words—"feel good
inside."

Orson shook the spider off, and dust clouded his
face. "Be careful! You were sent to observe, not
to get involved."

Mork snapped to attention. "Yes, sir!" He bent
over and twisted his ears. "This is Mork signing
off from Boulder, Colorado. Until next week, *Na-
No, Na-No*."

And from the deepest reaches of Outer Space,
Orson answered, *"Na-No, Na-No,"* leaving Mork
to face the confused and horribly clean world of
Earth.